ERIC LUPER

BiG SLICK

FARRAR, STRAUS AND GIROUX
NEW YORK

o 71810122

www.fsgkidsbooks.com

Library of Congress Cataloging-in-Publication Data
Luper, Eric.
    Big slick / Eric Luper.— 1st ed.
        p. cm.
    Summary: Unable to resist the lure of poker but reluctant to admit
his addiction, sixteen-year-old Andrew, a talented player who relies
on his mathematical skills to plan game strategy, risks friendship and
his parents' trust as he begins to take money from his father's business
to finance his secret gambling activities.
    ISBN-13: 978-0-374-30799-8
    ISBN-10: 0-374-30799-7
    [1. Poker—Fiction. 2. Gambling—Fiction. 3. Honesty—Fiction.
4. Interpersonal relations—Fiction. 5. Self-perception—Fiction.]
    I. Title.

PZ7.L979135 Big 2007
[Fic]—dc22
                                                          2006041341

To my catalyst—Elaine—and
my two rate-controlling steps—Ethan and Lily

BIG SLICK

POCKET ROCKETS
(two aces)

Pocket aces. Shushie dealt me two aces: a club and a diamond. It's the best starting hand possible. Not often do cards like that come along—once in 221 hands to be exact. In five hours of playing, it's my first pocket aces and probably my only one for the whole tournament.

I stare at my cards and try to be ice. Every fiber in me wants to smile, to jump up and down, to point my fingers in the air and wiggle my knees back and forth like a showboating wide receiver after a touchdown. But poker isn't about grandstanding; it's about patience, it's about cool. And it's about money—lots of it.

Am I looking at my cards too long? I let them snap down to the table and gaze at the faded felt. I think about the Novocain from the last time my mom took me to the dentist, and let my face go numb.

Jimmy Burke, the local vet, and Sam Barr, our mailman, fold. Mandy Zimmer, the tired-looking waitress from the diner, knocks a hunk of ash from her cigarette. A finger of smoke rises from the ashtray and collects in the hazy blanket above the motionless ceiling fan. Mandy's fingernails are ragged and gnawed away. She calls the two-thousand-dollar bet.

I slide two black chips in front of me. "Call."

Shushie Spiegel, owner of the illegal poker club beneath the pool hall and the closest thing I have to a poker mentor, looks at me over his glasses with one of those "you sure you want to do this?" expressions. Then he glances at his stack. "Raise." He puts eight thousand down, two to call plus six more. Cheech Lombardi, the manager at the bakery, and some new guy who calls himself Sparks both fold. So, it's just Mandy, Shush, and me with fifteen grand in the pot.

It's not really fifteen grand. The chips are just points. You could call them clams or shekels or credits; it doesn't matter. It costs five hundred dollars to get in the tournament, and each player starts out with twenty thousand in chips. With a forty-player cap, the poker room takes in twenty grand cash, half of which goes to the winner.

Mandy calls and tosses in six thousand. Her stack is starting to look short.

The action is to me, and I'm tempted to raise Shush right back, to go over the top, but then he'd know I was holding good cards and he might fold. I want to bleed him slowly.

"Call," I say.

I don't usually play No-Limit Hold 'Em. It's too volatile. Anyone can bet their whole stack at any time, which means you have to have the *cojones* to stand behind your cards each and every hand. You can lose it all at once. But this tournament was too hard to pass up. The winner takes home ten thousand dollars cash, enough to get the money back in the register at my father's dry-cleaning business and still have a whole heap left for myself.

Shushie burns a card off the top of the deck and turns the

next three—ace of hearts, two of hearts, and two of clubs. I flopped a full house, three aces and a pair of twos. My heart pounds in my throat, and I fight to keep my breathing slow and even. With a full boat, I have the best possible hand at the table unless someone's holding both the other twos. But any player with a brain between his ears would've folded a low pair before the flop. Four twos or a straight flush could beat me, but both are major long shots.

Mandy peeks at her cards again, and I know she's holding two hearts. It's one of her tells. She does it every time she's four to a flush. She's looking to see if the hearts she's holding are high enough to stay in. Mandy drags on her cigarette so hard it crackles like a campfire. She taps the table, signifying a check. She wants to see cards cheap in the hope her fifth heart will come along. If it does, she'll go all in. But she's already dead in the water.

Shushie, on the other hand, is less readable. His eyes don't quite point in the same direction, and his brambly, graying beard covers most of his face. He's slippery, too. He never plays a hand the same way twice. Shushie stares at me over his horn-rims. The burst capillaries on his bulbous nose make an intricate spiderweb that even the most talented team of spiders would have trouble spinning. "You gonna play or just sit there?" he says.

I glance at the others who've already folded. I scan the dozens of spectators. I love the feeling of all these people hanging on me. Me, Andrew Lang, high school junior. I only have my learner's permit, but here I am at the poker club making them all nervous. I inhale deeply. Breathing in the smoky air makes me feel older, more confident.

"I bet twenty thousand," I say. I push four white chips forward.

"Interesting," Shushie says. He leans back in his chair. It protests under his weight. "I'll raise another twenty." He tosses eight white chips in front of him.

Twenty thousand? Why did he raise twenty thousand? It's a small raise for the stack he's sitting on. It's certainly not enough to scare me off after my own twenty-thousand-dollar bet. A trap—it has to be a trap. Shushie taught me all about limping in, feigning weakness, and then following it up with a big bet to catch your opponent off guard. But I'm the heavy favorite in this hand.

"Too rich for my blood," Mandy says. She tosses her cards in. Even though her hand is promising, right now she's got nothing.

It's just me and Shush now, and the action is to me.

When I was new to poker, I would've freaked out at spending five hundred bucks on a single tournament. I would have said to myself, *Jeez, think of all the cool stuff I could buy with that money: a bunch of PlayStation games, a kick-ass snowboard and boots, a hundred Supersize Extra Value Meals at McDonald's.* I would've turned down the game without a second thought and spent the night hanging out with Scott. Now, a year later, I don't even flinch. I've lost twice that in one shot. I've also made more than five times that in the same amount of time. The one thought that runs through my head now is: *If I don't put it out there, I'll never win.*

"Play already," Shushie grumbles. "Stop sitting there like a lump of crap."

He's trying to intimidate me. That might've worked a few months ago, but I've learned a lot since then. The minimum bets are going up in a few minutes, though, so the faster I play the cheaper I can play for. When the blinds go up, the scales tip toward the players with the largest stacks. I pick at a crusty glob on the felt for a few seconds just to get under his skin.

"Call," I say and match his bet.

Shushie burns another card and turns up a king of hearts — one step closer to a straight flush. My face gets a little hot, but the odds of him holding two good hole cards and hitting the last one on the river are about one in fifteen thousand.

I glance at my stack. I'm sitting on about two hundred thousand in chips, around a quarter of the total for the tournament. If I were playing limit poker like I usually do, I'd be stoked. I'd walk away right now and consider early retirement. But the dollar amount on the chips means nothing. In tournament play, everyone has to keep going until one player has it all.

Shushie has close to twice what I have. I can't bump him out no matter what, but I could wound him. I might cripple the best player at the table. I can be chip leader and gain control of the action. With the betting limits going up soon, that would be huge. I could pick off the other players one by one.

And if I win, I can get that money back into the register.

And I'll have a big bankroll, so I can play the higher stakes tables next week.

Stop thinking like that. This is the right bet to make. There won't be an opportunity like this for the rest of the night. My heart explodes over and over again at the base of my throat. This is the turning point of the tournament. I'm going to remember this hand for a long time.

I slide my entire stack to the center of the table.

"All in," I say.

CRABS

(two threes)

The report of Jasmine's staple gun snaps me out of my daze. "You look like hell," she says as she fastens a dry-cleaning tag to the label of a linen blazer.

"Yeah, thanks." I can't get the tournament out of my head. Four of a kind. Shushie had four of a freaking kind. A pair of deuces on the table and two in his hand. I run the scenario over and over again in my head. Odds were 1 in 946 that he was holding those cards. He should have folded before the flop.

"It was the right hand to play," Shushie called to me as I made my way out of the poker club. "It was the smart bet." His words echoed in my head long after they dissipated in the concrete stairway. Hell, they're still echoing in my head now. If it was the right bet, why do I feel like such an idiot?

"What's the matter?" Jasmine asks me.

"Uh, I didn't get much sleep last night."

"*Star Trek* marathon or something?"

I ignore her.

"Gross," Jasmine squeals. She drops a small lavender packet and the navy blue pants to the counter as though they're on fire.

"What?" I accidentally staple the numbered tag through the collar of the silk blouse in my hands.

"Condom alert!" Jasmine grabs a wire hanger, lifts Mr. Daniels's pants by the belt loop, and drops them into the bin. "I hate checking people's pockets. It's nasty."

"Yeah, but then we wouldn't have our Cross pen collection or our Chinese food fund." I rattle the collection can. "We might have enough for moo shu pork soon."

Jasmine wrinkles her nose and finishes tagging Mr. Daniels's clothes, touching as little of the fabric as possible.

"Anyhow," I say, "what's worse is thinking about Mr. Daniels having sex."

"Yuck. He's like fifty." Jasmine punches me in the shoulder. One of her rings catches my shirt and pulls a little loop of thread free.

Jasmine might not be the kind of girl you'd see in *Glamour*, but I think she's hot: short black hair that probably took an hour to make look messy, a dozen or so silver earrings in her ears, a nose ring, a tongue barbell, and a pale, round face with a ton of eyeliner. At first, people are scared of her because she's sort of a Goth, but once you get to know Jasmine, watch out. She's infectious.

I take the wire hanger and prod the condom wrapper. I read from the packaging: "Ribbed for Her Pleasure."

"Double yuck," she says. "If I get to triple yuck I'm gonna hurl all over you."

Jasmine and I tackle the rest of the tagging. Each gray nylon sack holds one customer's clothing. Each bundle receives a different numbered tag, and each article of clothing is tagged with the same number. That way, we can separate each order after the clothes come out of the machines and get pressed. Once the clothes get tagged, we toss them into the bins. The white bin is for three days out. Red is for rush. Yellow is for special care stuff. I keep telling my dad to get a computer system. It would do all the work for us. But he figures a computer will screw everything up.

I sneak a glance at Jasmine. She's wearing a tuxedo shirt rolled up to her elbows. The top three buttons are undone, and I can see the red lace of her bra peeking out at me. She's not thin, for sure—nothing like the supermodels in all the magazines—but boy does she have curves.

"Let me know when you're done staring," she says.

My face flushes and my eyes dart down to the countertop. "You swipe that shirt from the unclaimed clothes rack?"

"My other one got all dirty in the back," she says. "Anyhow, this shirt's been hanging here for like two years."

"I don't care," I say. And really, I don't. I'm just glad I recovered so well from getting snagged. When I sneak a glance a few minutes later, only two buttons are undone.

The bell over the door jingles.

"Hey, dork," Scott says to me. "Hey there, Jaz."

Jasmine smiles and goes back to tagging.

Scott and I have been buddies since sixth grade, when he moved here from Cincinnati. He doesn't have many friends, so he spends a lot of time at work with me. His parents are divorced, and his dad gives him enough money to keep him happy, the lucky bastard.

Scott takes off his jacket and boosts himself onto the counter. His sneakers drum against the side of it one after the other. *Thump, thump, thump.* "Wanna play cards tonight?" he asks.

At the word *cards* my stomach knots up like someone is twirling around my intestines with a spaghetti fork. But Scott isn't talking about poker. He's talking about Four Horsemen, a fantasy card game we started playing years ago. It's what got me so into cards in the first place. I discovered I was pretty good at tumbling the odds around in my head and manipulating the numbers. It wasn't much of a leap to poker after I saw a few tournaments on cable. With poker I can win money.

Scott snaps his fingers in front of my face. "I'm talking to you, dork."

"You're calling me a dork? You're the one wearing yellow sweatpants and a purple shirt with an airbrushed wizard on it."

A sharp squeal of laughter bursts from Jasmine. She stifles it just as quickly as it came out.

Scott pulls his shirt flat with both hands and looks down. "Yellow and purple match. It's like the Minnesota Vikings."

"Yellow and purple do not match. They're on opposite sides of the color wheel."

Scott looks down at himself again. "What do you think, Jasmine?"

"They match okay, I guess."

"Yeah," I say. "That's coming from someone whose idea of a varied wardrobe is jet black, pitch black, and ink black."

Jasmine meets my gaze. "What about red?"

My face flushes as red as her bra. "I can't play tonight. Homework."

"Homework, or you're otherwise occupied?" When Scott says "otherwise occupied," he makes those little quotation marks in the air with his fingers and it makes him look like a moron. Scott knows I play poker. He's been good about keeping my secret, even though he's always on my case about stopping. Anyway, he doesn't complain after I have a good night and I buy him stuff—CDs, T-shirts, and all sorts of other crap—at the mall. Hell, he's cashed in pretty good these past few months.

"No, really," I say. "I have a ton of homework tonight."

Scott narrows his eyes and I wing a sweater at him to wipe the smirk off his face. The sweater wraps around his head like a hungry octopus.

"Go change the music," I tell him.

Scott makes his way over to the radio perched on top of the pay phone. He rolls the dial off the lame oldies station my dad listens to and tunes in the hip-hop station. Jasmine starts bobbing to the beat.

"Jim is obsessed with this song," she says.

Jim is Jasmine's dirtbag boyfriend. I hate when she talks about him. It gets my skin all crawly. Jim graduated two years ago and still hangs out at the convenience store across from the high school. I'm pretty sure that he's a dealer. Sometimes he gives Jasmine a ride to work and I want to huck rocks at his canary yellow Integra.

"Put it on soft rock," I say. "My dad'll freak if he comes back and Ludacris is rapping about niggas and bitches."

"Just more evidence you're a dork," Scott says. He changes the station and heads for the door. "I gotta run. My dad told me I have to rake today or he's gonna crush my head in his vise. There's a snowstorm coming this weekend." He knocks on the counter to get my attention. "But hey, if you change your mind about cards, I'll be home tonight." The door jingles and slams behind him.

I shake my head and get back to tagging.

"He's funny," Jasmine says.

"Yeah, as funny as a brain tumor."

"What game is he talking about?"

"Oh, just some card game we've been playing since we were kids." Jasmine is a senior, and if she finds out I play Four Horsemen, she'll laugh her head off. Aside from ten-year-olds with Harry Potter hats, the only people who play it are owners of comic book shops and other card-carrying members of the nerd herd.

"And what's 'otherwise occupied' mean? You have a girlfriend or something?"

"No," I say too quickly. My face gets hot again.

Jasmine and I finish tagging clothes in silence. It takes until four-thirty.

"Mind if I work the register for the rush today?" I ask. Jasmine usually takes the register while I retrieve the clothes from the automated rack or from the unfiled stuff next to the pressing machines.

"You know I hate lugging all the orders up from the back," Jasmine whines. "The hangers dig into my hands."

When she pouts, I fix on her dark lips. I almost agree to let her cash out the customers. Then reality sets in. I have to balance the drawer or my dad is going to notice the missing five hundred dollars. Fortunately, it's Thursday and we'll likely do somewhere near two grand before closing.

"I twisted my ankle last night taking out the garbage," I say. "How about I'll do all the sweeping up? Once the rush is over, you can jet out early."

"You do all the sweeping every day anyway. Plus, how're you going to sweep if you hurt your ankle?"

"If I sit on the stool for the next few hours, I'll save up my energy."

She puts her hands on her waist and thrusts one hip out. Jasmine knows exactly how to make black-and-white striped leggings and Doc Martens look good. "Okay," she says. "But I think you're full of it."

As the customers come, I hit Cash Out without entering the total but still put the money in the drawer. That way, the dollars don't ring onto the tape and I can make up for the five hundred I took yesterday. I don't do it with every customer, just the ones I figure won't notice: old people, women with screaming kids, men in a rush, and anyone with a car worth more than forty grand.

I tuck the receipts under the register, keeping track of the invoice numbers and running total. That way, I can balance the books when I replace the money later. As long as I get every cent back in the drawer by the end of the month, I'll be fine. My luck is bound to change by then.

By six-thirty, the rush is over. Jasmine hoists her backpack onto her shoulder. "I'm gonna blast out of here," she says, chewing on a big wad of gum. She blows a pink bubble almost as big as her head, and it bursts across one cheek. "Have fun cleaning up."

I thrust my chin at her in a classic guy acknowledgment. "Later." I watch her walk out. God, even her calves are amazing.

I grab the broom and push it around the floor. Behind the pressing machines and under the racks can wait until Saturday. My father will never notice the dust back there.

I hear two car doors slam in close succession. Then the

back door swings open and slams against the building. Rooster, my five-year-old brother, darts in and winds between the bagged clothes like a heat-seeking missile. Over his sweatshirt, he's wearing a bright yellow Wilkes Regional High School varsity girls' basketball T-shirt that hangs down to his knees. It says LADY YELLOWJACKETS in blue block letters.

"Andrew!" Rooster screams as he shoulder-tackles me.

I make a show of rolling backward into the clothing bin like a Mack truck hit me. Rooster's real name is Jeffrey Oliver Lang, but I've called him Rooster since he was a baby and I told my mother his crying sounded like a sick rooster. "Hey, Roo, what's going on?"

"Nothing much. Dad's all grumpy on account of cuz we lost again." Rooster smiles up at me. His metal-framed glasses make him look like he's got a perpetual squint.

Another loss. Not a good thing. My father's mood hinges on the success of the fifteen or so games of the season, and we're 0 and 7. I climb out of the clothing bin and hear my father trotting in. Even though he only wears sneakers, his footsteps sound like he's got military boots on.

"Everything okay around here?" he asks.

"Fine."

"I don't know why I coach that team in the first place. They don't do a goddamn thing I tell them."

Rooster giggles at my father's creative use of language.

Despite the cold, my father only has a team T-shirt on. He lumbers like a silverback gorilla straight to the register. My arm hair stands at attention.

"What do those parents expect?" he asks me as he thumbs through the cash drawer. I'm not quite sure if he's waiting for an answer, so I don't say anything. I know I failed him in seventh grade when I refused to go off to basketball camp and fulfill his dream of me becoming a superstar jock. I just can't get jazzed up about bouncing a big ball around and tossing it into a hoop. I think he coaches the girls' team to make some sort of twisted point: *Even girls can play basketball.*

I keep my head down and follow the broom back to the storage room. The vapors from the barrels of dry-cleaning fluid burn my nose. It feels like someone jammed ice picks into my sinuses, but it's nothing compared with my father when he goes ballistic.

"Need any help?" Rooster asks, poking his head in.

"Out," I say. "You know you're not allowed back here with all the fumes."

"Dad won't care. I'm gonna have to come back here sometime. I'm gonna start working here soon. He said I could come in some days over the summer. How many months away is that?"

"You don't want to work here."

My father's voice sounds like thunder from the front of the store. "Goddammit!" he yells. "We took in shit today."

Rooster giggles again. "He said shit!"

"Zip it," I hiss. Then I call to my father, "We did a bunch of credit cards." My sinuses really start to sting from the chemicals.

"We're around six hundred short of a regular Thursday!"

"Wow," Rooster says. "Six hundred dollars. That's close to a million."

I lay a hand on my front pocket. *I need that extra hundred dollars. Seed money.*

A J A X
(an ace and a jack)

Shushie sits crammed behind his desk in the tiny office in the rear of the poker room. And when I say *crammed*, I don't mean it looks like he gently slid himself behind the desk. It looks like six guys came in with grease and a few crowbars to wedge him back there and it would take a Jaws of Life to get him back out. The edge of the desk presses into his gut so hard that even I have trouble breathing.

He spreads his welcoming arms wide. Sweat circles under his armpits turn his maraschino cherry red polo shirt a deep crimson. "What can I do for my favorite poker prodigy?" he says. His voice sounds like steel shovels scooping gravel.

"Shushie, I —"

"I know." He takes a puff on his cigar and blows the smoke out the side of his mouth. It filters through the metal grating of the cash window facing the card room. Shushie doesn't use the cash window except on big money nights, like yesterday's tournament, or when there are a lot of strange faces playing. The cage wall with the rectangular slot reminds me of the drug rooms in the insane asylums I've seen in movies.

"You're upset about losing your first tournament," Shushie says. He watches the smoke glide through the grating. "We all lose our first tournament, kiddo. It's all part of the process."

"I had pocket—"

"Yeah, pocket aces. Tough break." The smoke rising from the ashtray spins in bluish gray eddies and whorls. "You should've bet bigger before the flop. Would've scared me off before my quads came around. You got a little greedy, that's all."

"But—"

"I know, I was sitting right there." Shushie grins, exposing his small, pearly yellow teeth. "It was a bad beat, but you played great poker last night," he says. "For Crissakes, I never expected you to make it past the first table. No Limit is nothing like the small-time stuff you usually sit in on. It's a different animal, kiddo—no offense—different betting structures, different starting hands, everything. And it ain't like what you see on television either. It's a whole new ball game when you can't see what the other guy's got." Shushie's eyes move over the local paper spread across his desk under a few Chinese food containers and a heavy ceramic mug that says HORNY BASTARD on it.

"Speaking of ball games," he says. "How'd your dad do today?"

"Lost."

"Damn, I had high hopes for those girls once your father took that team over. He's a great coach, you know. Was a great player in high school, too."

I nod, barely listening. I've heard the story about my father's dashed basketball dreams about a thousand times. About how all the big schools were coming around, watching him play, until he busted his ankle in the state tournament.

"Those girls have to get their act together—learn to work like a team."

My mind is reeling, but I'm determined not to let him change the subject. I came to talk about poker, but Shushie is a master of pushing a conversation wherever he wants. I bring it back. "About last night—"

"Look, kiddo," he says. He leans forward, and his red polo shirt bulges over the lip of the desk like a lard-filled balloon. "Knowing the odds is one thing. Playing the game is another. Pocket aces don't mean shit. All pocket aces means is that you have a better chance of winning the hand than any other single player at the table. In fact, even with pocket aces, you're still the underdog against the rest of the field." He leans back, and his chair thumps against the cinder-block wall. "And hell, I got damned lucky. Four deuces." He grins wider than an oyster. "Not often does a hand like that come along."

"I lost five hundred bucks," I say. I kick the tip of my sneaker against the corner of his metal desk. It makes a louder sound than I expected and I jump.

Shushie closes his eyes and shakes his head. "Gamblers win and gamblers lose. Get used to the highs and lows."

It's the first time anyone's ever called me a gambler, and my insides clench like a tightly wrung dishrag. I'm not a gambler; I'm more of a numbers guy—a statistician. Command of the odds is what gives me my edge. And with an edge like that I know I'll win money over time. It's just a matter of getting back on my feet. And getting that money back in the register.

Shushie exhales through his nose like a bull about to charge. "We talked about this before the tournament. You assured me you had a big bankroll—that you'd been saving up and it was no problem."

I look down at my lap.

"I think the words you used were 'I have enough squirreled away.' You already lying to support your habit?"

"It's not a habit," I say. "I'm good at poker."

"You are," Shushie says. He takes a sip from his mug and chokes a mouthful down. "Shit coffee," he mutters. "I gotta learn how to use that damn coffeemaker. I got a grinder back there and everything. Look, you're the best kid I've seen come through here in a long time, but you have to have patience. Pace yourself and don't get in over your head."

In a long time? I never thought about it before. I guess I assumed that I was the only kid—unique—that no one as young as me played here. "There've been others my age?"

"Plenty of them." He flips a thumb toward the poker room. "Cheech. Guy Chawalski. Sammy Barr. Hell, Sammy's been playing since he was fourteen. He started out spending his paper route money here."

Tired, overweight, ashen—the thought of myself becoming like them flits through my mind. And just as quickly, I push the thought away. I'll never be like them.

"Look, Shush," I say. I fish the five twenties out of my pocket and lay the crumpled bills on the table. "I was wondering if you'd start up a one–three table for me. Maybe a three–six. Just this once. I have to make my money back."

Shushie rolls his wet, chewed cigar around in the ashtray. "No can do," he says.

"Come on, Shush. I . . ."

Shushie glares at me, and I stop talking. He sucks on his cigar, and the tip glows orange. He speaks through the dense smoke that floats out of his mouth and hovers around his head. "If I started a low-limit table for every guy who lost his wad the night before, I'd be out of business. Half the people at the ten–twenty table would move over. It'd kill my rake."

Shushie's been running this place a long time. He's friendly enough, but with him it always comes down to money. Starting a $1–$3 table would reduce the amount the poker room took in by lowering the 10 percent rake Shushie takes from every pot. But if I sit at a $10–$20 table with a hundred in chips, it'll eat through my stack quick.

Shushie hoists himself out of his chair and squeezes around the desk. He puts a hand on my shoulder. A hand on the shoulder means *end of discussion*. "Look, kid," he says. "I know what you're going through. I've seen it a hundred times before. Hell, I've been there myself. Let me give you some advice."

My shoulders tense. I don't need a lecture.

"Stop playing cards." As he talks, his cigar hangs from his lip like it's glued there. "Quit. Walk away. You're a good kid with a bright future. Don't end up like all the other assholes out there."

This is not what I need to hear.

"Look, Shush, I—"

Shushie holds a hand up to silence me. "Don't put me in this position. You get in over your head and all of a sudden I'm the bad guy. What happens when you get in deeper? I'll tell you what happens. It comes back to me. Your dad calls the cops or comes down here with a baseball bat. I don't need that kind of headache."

Shushie sits back down and sweeps the Chinese food containers into the garbage with his arm. He picks up his newspaper and rattles it to attention. "You see this? Some guy punched his girlfriend's eighteen-month-old kid to death. Jesus Christ."

Shushie's reading me the paper. Conversation definitely over. "How much did you win last night?" I ask.

Shush looks at me over his glasses. "Huh?"

"How much was the final jackpot?"

"A little over ten grand," he says, looking back down.

"Wow." I don't think I've ever seen that much cash at once. "Shush, I'm not a hundred percent clear. Am I cut off?"

Shushie pinches the bridge of his nose over his glasses. He squeezes his eyes closed like he is trying to push away a migraine. "Nah," he sighs. "You're not cut off."

I jam my hand back into my pocket and pull out my twenties. I drop them on the desk. "Let me get some chips then."

"You know a hundred's not enough," Shushie says. "You'll burn through it before anything comes your way."

"All I need to do is catch a few good cards. It's worth a shot."

Shushie smirks his disapproval and sweeps the bills into the cashbox. He puts eighteen five-dollar chips down, and I scoop them into a Lucite chip caddy. I forgot about the ten-dollar sitting fee. Eighteen measly chips. I better make them count. I turn to the poker room when I hear Shushie.

"Wasn't me."

"Huh?" I say as I turn around.

"Wasn't me who won the tournament."

"Who did?"

"Mandy," Shushie says. "She had a run of great cards and knocked us all out one by one. Took me with a ten-high straight to my two pairs."

"Jeez." The chips in my hand suddenly feel heavier.

"It happens."

"Where's Mandy now?" I ask, peering out of the office. "I didn't see her when I came in. I should congratulate her."

"She won't be back until she smokes it up."

"Smokes what up?"

"You got a lot to learn, kiddo."

JEFFREY DAHMER

(an eight and a jack)

There are two open $10–$20 Hold 'Em tables running. I stand back and watch the action. Sometimes choosing the right seat is the difference between a great night and a horrible night. You have to look at how many players are at each table and how loose the betting is. Once you pick a table, you have to try to keep the aggressive and very good players to your right so you know what they do before it's your turn. You should also try to keep the bluffers and passive players to your left because it lets you check-raise more. Check-raising helps you beef up the pot when you're holding good cards.

Shush once told me that picking the right seat in the poker room is half the game.

I think it's more than that.

"Hey, Andrew," a voice snaps. I look up. Matt LeRou, a math major at St. Benedict College, is waving his hand for me to move out of the way. "You're blocking the game."

I glance at the television and shuffle to the side. The prehistoric set, covered in a half inch of dust, is on top of an old filing cabinet. A black horizontal line flickers up and down across the hockey game, making the puck all but impossible to follow.

For the first time since I started coming to the poker

room, it feels stifling in here. The stench of nervous sweat and greasy steak sandwiches invades my nostrils. The walls squeeze in on me.

I slide between Joe "Cap" Capadonna and Pete Granger. From what I can tell, it's the best available spot in the poker room. Pete is a real tight player—probably because he's an accountant. They're trained to be tight with money. Cap is much more aggressive and much more experienced than me. Best to have him play before me.

"How's it going?" Pete asks me. He peers at his two cards and tosses them to the center of the table. "Heard about the tournament last night. Tough break."

"Yeah, too bad," says Sam from the other side of the table. "I got bumped right after you. Mandy was on fire."

I purse my lips and nod.

"Shushie has got to change those tournament rules," Sam says. "Everyone at the final table should get a payout, not just the top three."

"Yeah," I say and place my chips in front of me. My stack is the smallest at the table. Everyone knows I am going to be looking for a big score early on. They'll attack me like starving hyenas. I'm going to have to play a little recklessly and take the first playable cards that come along.

Everyone folds, and Mary Church, sitting in the big blind this hand, scoops the pot. The button moves to the left and the dealer shuffles up.

I place two chips, ten dollars, in front of me. In Texas Hold 'Em, you have to put money out on the table only if you are one of the two seats to the left of the player holding the button. It's called being in the blind. The button, which is actually a big white disk the size of a peanut butter jar lid, moves to the left at the end of every hand and travels clockwise around the table. That way, not everyone has to ante every hand. Even though I'm not in the blind yet, if you sit down in the middle of a rotation, you have to put money out there anyway. It's to prevent people from walking away when the button comes around and then sitting back down after it's passed.

The sharp clicking of chips being stacked and tossed around rings in my ears. There's something about that sound that gets me going. I swing the bill of my baseball cap around from the back to the front to shade my eyes a little.

"Guess it's time for business," Sam says, pointing to my cap. He's still wearing his postman shirt, and his bushy mustache partially hides his grin.

A few seats to my left, Ben Huxley, one of Matt's college buddies, tugs the hood of his sweatshirt farther over his head. He's a marginal player—good enough to have a few big nights here and there but not nearly good enough to make a living playing poker. "Wish it worked," he says, pointing to my cap, too. "I'd run out and buy myself one. I'm down a buck fifty tonight."

I survey the table and do the math. With seven other players, if I continually fold without a bet I can survive for thirty-five hands before the antes eat up my entire stack. It might seem like a lot of poker, but it's not. It's less than an hour of play. It's five trips of the button around the table. And if I don't act soon, my stack'll be so small that even doubling up would leave me short of where I started. I figure I need to make a move before the eleventh hand is dealt. And bluffs are not going to work; whatever hand I play, these guys are going to take me all the way to the river.

The good news is that, with eight players, odds are I'll have the best starting hand at least once in eleven hands, maybe twice. The trick is figuring out which hands they are and then maximizing the money in the pot on those hands.

My first two cards come—a nine and a five off suit. Players call it a Dolly Parton. Shushie told me it was because of a movie she was in once. Whatever. Card players have all sorts of weird names for poker hands—Jack Benny, Blocky, Beer Hand. I guess all that sitting around leaves plenty of time for two things: watching your ass get fatter and making up names for card hands. And the two are not mutually exclusive.

Anyhow, a nine and a five off suit is a terrible starting hand. Since my ante is already on the table, I check. If no one else raises, I get to see the flop for free, and that could turn everything around.

One by one, players fire their cards to the center of the table. Mary Church calls the big blind, and Sam taps the table—a check. So, it's Mary, Sam, and me for the flop. The three cards come. All garbage.

I tap the table and quickly fold after Sam's ten-dollar raise. Mary folds, too, and Sam grabs the forty-dollar pot.

I'm down from ninety to eighty dollars in a snap.

"Wanna go out to the casino this weekend?" Matt asks Ben.

"I have a medieval history test on Monday."

"I'll help you study in the car."

"Yeah, like that'll happen. Your head will be buried in some poker book."

After the shuffle, Ben passes the button to Mary. Mary blows my mind. She's a stay-at-home mom. How she gets out every night to play poker I have no idea. And she's not the only mom here who plays regularly. My mother, on the other hand, stays home except for her monthly book group, when a bunch of biddy old ladies sit around each other's living rooms, sip chardonnay, and gab about anything but the stupid book.

"What casino?" I ask Matt.

"An Indian casino about an hour and a half from here."

"You mean Crystal Waters? I see commercials for that place all over the television."

"That's the place."

"I thought it was like four or five hours away."

"Nope."

The next two deals bring me trash and I fold. Matt stole the first hand with a pair of nines. I would've won that one with a straight had I stayed in, and it burns me up a little even though it was only a thirty-five-dollar pot. Felix Mancino, the owner of the Italian restaurant across from my dad's store, won the next hand with two pairs, queens and eights. He played it great and ended up with ninety dollars more than he started with. Since I'm not in the blind, those hands are free. I am still at eighty dollars.

It's a good thing players at Shushie's club are discreet. Otherwise, Felix would have said something to my father long ago. They are both active in the Chamber of Commerce and love to talk all the time about how bad business is.

Shushie makes it clear that one screwup gets you banned forever, and he's the only real game in town. No one says a word.

"Hey," I say to Matt. "I'll go to Crystal Waters with you. I'd love to check it out."

"What're you, like fifteen?"

"Sixteen."

"No way," Matt says. "I'm shooting for twenty hours at the table. If you get carded . . ."

The next hand puts me in the big blind. I ante my ten dollars and feel a trickle of sweat roll down the small of my back. I should have waited for the button to pass before sitting down. I should have risked losing the seat to someone else. But it's too late for "I should've." After my ante, I'm down to seventy bucks.

Mary touches a photo of her kids, which is lying on the felt in front of her. She puts her fingers on that photo before every hand. "Good luck," she says to me.

I smile my thanks.

Rosie tosses my cards to me with the accuracy of Annie Oakley. Rosie is my favorite dealer and a permanent fixture in the poker room. Come to think of it, I don't recall ever seeing her even take a bathroom break. She must be a machine. The two cards slip under my ante like she tucked them there by hand. Everything in me wants to look at what cards are lying there, but I know to wait until my turn comes. It was a hard habit for me to break, but I don't want to risk giving any information to the other players before I have to. Sam Barr's got a knack for reading faces, and he's almost directly across from me.

Pete and Felix both fold. Ben calls, followed by Mary. Sam folds, as does Matt. To my right, Cap calls my big blind and raises another ten. I flip up the corner of each card and let them snap back down to the faded felt. A king and ten of clubs. Promising cards. Nothing great, but promising. I match Cap's raise. Ben and Mary call, too.

Eighty bucks in the pot, only twenty of which is mine. But my stack is down to sixty. I'm limping bad.

The flop comes—ace of clubs, ten of hearts, and five of clubs. That puts me in a decent position. I'm sitting on a pair of tens with four cards to a flush. That means I'm holding an okay hand with fourteen cards in the deck that would give me a strong one. My fourteen outs are any other club (there are nine of them), which would give me the nut flush; one of three kings, which would give me two pairs; or one of two tens, which would give me three of a kind. With two cards coming, I have just over a 50 percent chance of hitting one of my outs.

Now I have to think. What potential hands could beat me? Right now, anyone holding one or more aces, two fives, or two tens has the advantage. Chances are that one of the other players—Ben, Mary, or Cap—is holding an ace, but considering how good my chances are of hitting a big hand, staying in is real attractive.

Cap goes first. He takes a ten-dollar chip from his stack and places it in front of him. Between last turn and this one, Cap is betting strong. It makes me nervous, but I'm already twenty dollars into this hand. Ten dollars more for an eighty-dollar pot with more than a 50 percent chance of hitting a great hand is the smart bet. It's one to one that I'll make eight times my investment. It's not a sure thing, but it's the right play.

I put two five-dollar chips out. And as soon as I do, I regret it. I should have raised and scared the other guys off the pot. I'm such a goddamn amateur! I made the same mistake at the tournament last night. Everyone else is waiting to catch cards, too, and if I give them the chance, it could knock me out of the box.

Ben calls. Then Mary folds. So much for rubbing her kids' faces.

Now there's a hundred and ten in the pot. If I win, it's about a 50 percent return on my total investment—not bad for a few minutes' work.

"You ready for this?" Cap says. He wiggles a French fry around in the puddle of ketchup on his plate and jams it in his mouth. "You ready to put it all on the line on this hand?"

I don't answer his table chatter. Cap's looking for a response, anything to glean what cards I'm holding. I fight a smirk from rising on my face and lower my eyes to the felt. *Did I just reveal something by looking down?* I stare at an ant feasting on a crumb next to my ten remaining poker chips. I consider squashing him but decide to let him live. I don't need the bad karma.

"Good luck," Rosie says to no one. She deals the next card. The fourth card, the one after the flop, is called the turn. It's a jack of spades. No help to me. Actually it hurts. If either Cap or Ben is holding a jack, he has the advantage. Plus it's one less chance for my fourteen outs to come. My odds just went from over 50 percent to around 25. Poker is a game of numbers, and the scales just tipped away from me.

Cap checks, and I tap the table, too.

I see Shushie watching me. He's leaning in the doorway to his office, his coffee mug in hand.

Ben fingers his stack and hunches forward in thought. I can see only a crescent of his face peeking out from his hood. For the turn and the river, bets go up to twenty dollars. I can tell he's considering whether he should push me.

"I'll let it slide this time," he says, and at that instant I know he has bad cards. He's waiting on something. I put him on an ace-high inside straight draw. That gives him an 8.5 percent chance to catch his last card on the river—a long shot. Like I said before, Ben is a marginal player. He'd rather stay in to keep you honest than make the smart move. For him, the smart move would be to fold.

I watch the little ant nibbling away.

Rosie snaps her gum between her teeth. It crackles like a wet log in the fireplace. She flips the last card up. It's a king of diamonds. My chest pounds. I just hit a second pair. That's great, but I still have to figure out what the other guys might be holding. A flush is impossible with only two spades on the board. A queen would give someone a straight, but would Ben or Cap have stayed in all this time with only a queen? Shit, I should have bet bigger earlier. *Focus, Andrew.* What could beat me? A pair of aces, tens, fives, jacks, or kings in hand would make three-of-a-kind. My hand doesn't look so good anymore.

The numbers tumble around in my head like balls in a bingo machine, but I know odds are bullshit now. The cards are already dealt. The reality is on the table and there's no point in calculating odds. It is what it is. I have fifty dollars left in my stack, five of which will go into the next hand's ante. The question I have to ask myself is: Am I likely to catch better cards on the very next hand or not?

The answer is no.

That means I'm doomed if I fold now.

Cap bets twenty, but it tells me nothing. He's too unpredictable a player. During one tournament, I heard he went all-in on a two-seven off suit, the worst starting hand possible, just to throw Guy Chawalski off. Cap is forcing my hand and I'm following right along.

Damn, I knew I should've bet bigger earlier. I know what has to happen now. I have no choice. I slide eight chips forward. "Raise."

"I raise another twenty," Ben says without a pause. He counts out sixty dollars in chips and drops them out in front of him.

Cap perks up. "You had that queen all along?" he says to Ben. "Son of a bitch." Cap tosses his cards in, and I know he is right. I'm screwed. I toss my last two chips into the pot.

Ben flips his cards over. A queen of hearts and a ten of diamonds. He hit the freaking straight.

I flip my cards over, and Ben's fists pump like those of an old-fashioned boxer. He rakes the $240 in chips toward himself.

"Nice job, dude," Matt says to Ben. They high-five over the table. "Good thing I folded that one. I would've been sucked in, too."

Shushie shakes his head and disappears into his office. The door slams shut.

"Sorry," Pete says and raps the table with his knuckles.

I think back to one of the first things I learned about

poker. It was before I ever spent a dime on it—when I was playing for free on the Internet. Just because a player sucks, it doesn't mean he's holding bad cards.

Ben got lucky.

I got burned.

Again.

To hell with karma. I smash the ant flat and get up from the table.

LITTLE PETE

(a two and a three)

Have you been smoking?"

The stench of the poker room is hard to shake off, even after pedaling the mile or so home with my jacket wide open.

"No," I tell my dad.

"Well, you stink like smoke." He hits Pause on the remote and freezes Sara Franzoni's three-point shot mid-arc. Replay films. He watches them after every game, not like it's helping any. "Don't let me find out you're smoking."

"I'm not."

His eyes narrow, and he scrutinizes me the way Shushie did right before I lost the tournament—like he was reading more than my words.

It's a miracle though. Usually, I don't rank high enough on my father's list of important things to merit pausing the replay video. The most I get from him when he's watching those tapes is a grunt with eyes still locked on the screen. My father's list of important things is as follows:

1. The "Big Three" professional sports—baseball, basketball, and football
2. His girls' basketball team, the Lady Yellowjackets

3. His blue 1970 Chevy Chevelle SS 454 (he named it Yoko)

4. Rooster (because he's starting to show some interest in sports and he helps my father wax the Chevelle sometimes)

5. Mom (because of all the cooking and cleaning she does)

6. A whole bunch of other shit

7. Me

Mom sets her wineglass on the coffee table and folds her crossword in half. "I'll warm up some dinner for you, Andrew."

"No thanks. Me and Scott went for a burger after the library." I know it's a lame lie, but it works. "I'll be up in my room."

"Well, how about a hot chocolate?"

Rooster leaps up from his nest of comic books on the couch. Bright yellow stars and moons cover his pajamas. "I want one!" he squeals and darts to the kitchen.

"The last thing you need is more sugar, Rooster," my mother says. "It's almost bedtime. How about some milk?"

"Chocolate milk?"

"Regular milk."

I follow my mother to the kitchen. She'll stare wide-eyed at her bedroom ceiling all night unless I let her fix me something.

"I better not find out you're smoking," my father calls after me. Cheering and static drown out his voice as the unpaused basketball game snatches his attention back.

Crisis averted.

In the kitchen, Rooster is playing with a chrome bottle opener that looks like a mermaid. Her tail opens the bottle. "Look, Andrew, boobies!"

"Rooster," Mom says. "Watch your mouth."

"*Boobies* is a bad word?"

Mom plucks the bottle opener from Rooster's fingers and hands him a cup of milk. "Carry it with both hands," she says and taps him on the bottom like a coach sending her player back into the game.

"No duh, Mom," Rooster says. His fuzzy bear-paw slippers scuffle across the tile as he goes out to the family room.

The swinging doors flap back and forth a few times, and Mom nukes a mug of water. I perch myself on a barstool at the counter and doodle a grid on the pad next to the phone. Then I start drawing an X in each square.

"Gail from my reading group tells me a bunch of kids from your class are going snowboarding over break." She dumps a packet of chocolate powder into the mug.

"I heard."

"Why don't you go with them?"

I shrug.

"Andrew," she says. She adds a few mini-marshmallows to the mix. "I want to talk to you about something."

Does she know about me playing poker? I leave my head down and continue making X's. I don't touch the mug she places in front of me.

"You know I don't like to harass you about school, but I got a call from Mr. David today."

School. She's talking about school. The boulder lifts off my shoulders and I gear up for the discussion.

"Mr. David," she says. "Your English teacher?"

"Yeah, I know."

"He said you're doing poorly this marking period."

"I don't like English."

"That's no answer, Andrew. You've never done poorly in school before—in any class." She taps her hand on the counter in my line of sight. "Look at me."

My gaze climbs up her sweatshirt to her face. Her deep-set eyes seem tired, almost weary. It's the first time I've ever looked at my mother and seen an older person. I've always looked at her as just Mom. It startles me, and I realize that even if my father is wrapped up in his lame excuse for a basketball career, Mom has a lot invested in Rooster and me. She doesn't have a job or much of a family. We're all she's got—us and her book group.

She levels her eyes to mine. "Andrew, are you doing drugs?"

"Mom, no! Jesus."

"I'm sorry, honey," she says and leans toward me across the counter. "With your grades . . . And you've been keeping weird schedules lately . . . And your clothes always stink like smoke . . ." She rambles like she's afraid to linger on any one thing too long, like somehow blurting it all out at once might make it less likely to be true. "It's just that if you were doing something like that, it would be okay to tell me. We could get you some help and—"

"Mom, I'm not doing drugs."

"Maggie Anderson's mom told me Maggie had some trouble like that. After some time up at Quiet Oaks—"

"Melville sucks, okay? Have you ever tried to read *Moby-*

Dick? I'm doing fine in all my other classes. Ask Mr. Ferris. Ask Mrs. Lamorges. I have an A in calculus."

"I know. I'm sorry, honey. It's just . . ." She pushes the mug toward me again, and I wrap my hands around it. My palms sting from the hot ceramic, but I welcome the pain. Mom purses her lips together and squeezes out a thin smile. "Promise me you'll work at getting that grade up and we won't mention it to your father."

"Okay."

Mom's eyes turn up and she looks like herself again. "I'd better get back out there," she says. "God forbid I miss a moment of that replay video." She pulls a beer from the refrigerator and pops the cap with the mermaid bottle opener. She holds up the bottle and wiggles it. "Dad's dessert."

A wave of guilt washes over me. Mom trusts me. Maybe I should tell her about the money—about the jam I'm in. The words push against the back of my teeth.

"Mom."

She stops and turns.

Just as quickly as the guilt came, it disappears and I know telling her would be the worst thing I could do. I stole from my father's store, but it's her store, too. "Thanks for the hot chocolate."

Her face warms. "Any time."

I sling my backpack over my shoulder, grab my mug, and retreat to my room.

The phone rings. I glance at the clock—10:41. It has to be Scott. I paw at the rumpled folds of my comforter for the cordless and click it on.

"What do you want?" I say.

"Quick. Turn on Channel Four."

"How come?"

"Just turn it on," Scott says. "There's a reality show called *Slimming the Sloth*. They're taking a bunch of fat people and making them work out."

"Sounds stupid."

"The weigh-in is after the commercial. You gotta see it."

"My dad's watching replay videos downstairs," I say, "and I hate going in my parents' room. It skeeves me out."

I grab Rooster's Slinky from my nightstand. I hold it by one end and lash it out like a whip. I try to knock over one of my sneakers, which is resting on the floor a few feet away. The Slinky makes a sound like a crashing cymbal. I miss and try again.

"Before the break," Scott says, "some fat guy swiped a bunch of chocolate cupcakes from the refrigerator and jammed them in his mouth. He had frosting and crumbs all over his face when the other team members walked in. Priceless."

"Why are there cupcakes in the house if they're supposed to be losing weight?"

"Temptation. It's part of the game. There's all sorts of junk food all over the place. One lady was crying about how it's not fair—about how hard it is to watch what she eats since she has to eat food every day. That's so lame."

I lash out the Slinky again. The sneaker wobbles and turns ninety degrees but doesn't tip over. "Maybe they can't help it."

"I don't understand that," Scott says. "I mean, how hard is it not to jam junk food in your mouth? Just say no, right?"

"I guess it's easy for us to say because we're not fat." I lie faceup across the bed. My head dangles off the edge toward the floor. The blood throbs behind my eyes, and I search out a new target for my Slinky whip.

"Gimme a break," Scott says. "Eating is an active process. You have to reach for the food and pick it up. Then you have to stick it in your mouth, chew, and swallow. Can't these people just put a little bit on their plate and not eat any more? What's that called? Portioning, I think."

"You know what else is an active process?" I say.

"What?"

"Picking up the handset, dialing my number, and chewing on my ear about ridiculous crap all the time."

"I have you on autodial," Scott says.

I fire the Slinky out again, this time at the pencil cup on my dresser. It strikes the nutcracker soldier my grandfather gave me the Christmas before he died. The nutcracker topples from the dresser and crashes to the floor. Pieces fly off, and the wooden body skitters under my desk.

"Shit, I gotta go."

"All right," Scott says. "The show's coming back on anyway. Wanna do something tomorrow night? Play some Four Horsemen? Maybe get some pizza delivered?"

"Sure. I'm tapped out, though."

"Don't sweat it. I'll grab a few twenties from my dad's drawer."

"Cool. See you tomorrow."

"Later."

"What the hell's that noise?" my father calls as he comes

up the stairs. He pounds on my door a few cursory times and opens it. "What's going on in here?"

"Nothing," I say. "I dropped something."

"What, you dropped something ten times? It sounds like you're hitting garbage cans with a golf club."

Rooster pokes his head into the doorway and darts around my father's legs. "My Slinky!" he says. Rooster grabs his toy, which is still hanging from my fingers like a dead snake. He squints up at me. Without his glasses, he looks much younger. "Boobies," he says. Then he giggles and heads out of the room.

"Try to keep it down," my father says to me. "You're getting your brother wound up." He pulls the door closed, and I hear him herd Rooster back to his room.

I pick up the remains of the nutcracker. His left arm is broken off, and his fuzzy jaw is split down the middle. I place the pieces in a pile on the dresser and take a sip of my hot chocolate.

It's already cold.

MIXED MARRIAGE

(an unsuited king and queen)

A **humming vibration** floats up from under the counter. Jasmine grabs her purse, pulls out her cell phone, and flips it open. "What do you want? You know I'm working . . . Uh-huh . . . Where is it? . . . Well, I can be ready by . . . Whatever." She snaps the phone shut. "Asshole," she mutters.

"What?"

"He's an asshole. Jim, I mean. He calls me just to get under my skin." Jasmine tosses her phone back into her pocketbook like it's covered in anthrax.

I like this conversation. "What'd he do?"

"He's going to a party tonight at his ex-girlfriend's house. I can tell he doesn't want me to go."

"Are you serious?"

"He didn't come out and say it, but I could tell. You know, the no-no-it's-fine-if-you-come-along bullshit. He's trying to piss me off so I'll stay home."

"What a jerk." I hate Jim even more, but at the same time, I'm ecstatic. Minus one point for Jim is plus one for me.

I shove one of the full bins with my hip. It glides to the back of the store and bumps lightly against the spotting station. I pull out all the clothes with bright orange stain stickers and leave them for my father to work on. The rest I toss into the dry-cleaning machine. "Why don't you dump the guy?" I ask.

"I don't know. I guess it's just easier to stay with him," Jasmine says. "I'd dump him if he gave me a reason, like if I actually caught him cheating on me or something."

I want to tell her she needs to dump him, but I'm afraid it'll come across like I want her, which I do. But then I'd be tipping my hand; I have to slow-play this one. "I could never date someone just because it's easy," I say. "It seems—I don't know—sort of lame."

"Easy for you to say, you're—" She stops and changes her tone. "You're probably right." Jasmine seems lost in thought, and I let her stay there while I pour the cleaning chemicals into the receptacle.

"How're you so good at calculus?" she asks. "I'm getting killed."

I can tell this is going to be one of those conversations where she compliments me and makes me feel like a nerd at the same time. I slam the machine closed and push the empty bin to the front. Jasmine is already tagging.

"I don't know," I say. "The numbers just come to me easy. It's like I can picture them in my mind. Does that make any sense?"

"You can picture derivatives and asymptotes in your head?" she asks with gallons of doubt in her voice.

"Don't you have something, like one thing, you're really good at?"

"No," Jasmine says, deadpan. She tosses an acetate blouse

into the red bin. It makes a swishing sound that sends shivers down my spine. I hate acetate. I can't figure out why women wear that stuff. It looks okay but feels like a chemical factory.

The heat from the pressing machine cooks the left side of my face. I reach behind the steam pipes and turn down the valve. We took in a lot of clothing yesterday, and my father insisted we run a few extra loads to catch up. Then he ran off to his precious team. Like always, I'm stuck finishing everything.

"Come on, there must be something," I say, glancing at Jasmine's outfit. She's wearing a tank top with a tight, long-sleeved, spiderweb-mesh shirt over it, a lace tier skirt, fishnet leggings, and knee-high boots. All black, of course—and all hot.

Jasmine grabs another nylon bag and dumps the contents on the counter. A purple satin gown and a tuxedo tumble out. "I suppose I'm good at scrapbooking," she says.

"You're good at what?"

"Scrapbooking," she says a little louder.

"That's a verb? Scrapbooking?"

"I don't know. They say it at the store I buy my supplies from."

"There are scrapbooking stores?"

"Craft stores. There are scrapbooking aisles, though. It's huge. Tons of people do it." She says that last part like she's trying to justify herself. I know what that feels like, so I lay off.

"But you're good at it. You like scrapbooking, right?"

"I guess," she says with a shrug.

"It's the same with me and math. I play around with the

numbers like you move the pictures and construction paper all over the pages."

Jasmine shrugs again. I can't tell if she's not interested or just uncomfortable talking about her hobby.

"You really make scrapbooks?"

"Yeah, why?" she says like if I push the issue any more, she'll bite my head off.

"I don't know. You just don't seem like the scrapbook type."

"What's the scrapbook type?"

I look at the ceiling as though the right words might be printed up there in big letters. Long dust tendrils hang from the vent. It amazes me that a place so dirty can actually get clothes clean. "I don't know—like Martha Stewart. She's the scrapbook type."

"I'm just like her," Jasmine says. "After a long day of scrap-booking, I like to make crab apple tarts and boysenberry pre-serves for my holiday banquet."

"What the hell's a boysenberry?"

"You got me." Jasmine pins a tag to the gown's label and moves to the tuxedo. "Isn't it weird for you to be in classes with all seniors?" She tosses the tagged jacket and pants into the spotting bin and grabs another bag. "Especially math—totally boring."

"There's a bunch of other juniors in class with me," I say. The words come out sounding defensive, and Jasmine abandons her line of questioning.

The silence grows between us.

"You need help with it?" I offer. My face gets hotter than when the steam was blasting. "With calculus I mean."

Jasmine looks up at me from her tagging, her eyes hopeful. "You wouldn't mind? This quiz on Monday is going to blow me out of the water."

I would help Jasmine with calculus if she charged me money, made me dress up like Betsy Ross, and told me to sing "The Star-Spangled Banner" on the front steps of the school. But I play it cool and lay out my biggest bluff ever. "Only if you promise to let me see your scrapbook."

"No way. There's a lot of personal stuff in there."

"That's my standard fee," I say. "Take it or leave it."

Jasmine's pencil-thin eyebrows disappear behind her bangs. "Looking at someone's scrapbook is your standard fee?"

I nod and put on my poker face, as blank and lifeless as a paper plate.

Jasmine smirks. "I'll tag. You start sweeping up. If your dad drops in and we're studying when there's still work to do, he'll freak out."

"What about the scrapbook?"

"I don't carry it around in my pocket. I'll bring it to work on Monday."

"Promise?"

"I promise."

I grab the broom and push it around the tile floor at a full sprint. I skip sweeping behind the machines and under the racks again. The dust can wait until tomorrow. A feeling of light-headedness swoops down on me, part from the dry-cleaning solvent and part from my excitement. I sweep the last specks out the back door and trot to the front. Jasmine is down to her last few bundles of tagging.

"Let's leave these," she says, poking her boot at the nylon bags. "We can grab them out of the bin and look busy if your father shows up."

"What about the bagging?" I point to the completed orders hanging on the racks. The clothing needs clear plastic pulled over it and the receipts stapled on.

"You can do those in the morning, right?"

Jasmine is dumping extra work on me, but I don't mind. Between sweeping, bagging, taking in orders, tagging the new stuff, and backing up the supplies, I'll be working until at least two tomorrow—on a Saturday. But it'll be worth every minute. "Sure." I feel like a puppy hopping around in a cage waiting to be picked up.

Jasmine pulls her calculus textbook from her backpack and spreads it open on the counter. The binding gives that never-been-opened crackle.

"You ever use this thing?"

"Once or twice," she says.

Her hip bumps against mine as she moves next to me, and I feel a tingle in the spot we touched. I glance at her face. It's the closest I've ever been to Jasmine. I shift out of her personal space. I don't want her to feel uncomfortable. Or maybe I don't want to feel uncomfortable myself.

Her eyeliner is too thick and a little sloppy. A fruity kind of scent invades my senses. The way she leans forward on the counter makes her cleavage strain against the spiderweb mesh of her shirt. I see it from the corner of my eye. All of a sudden, calculus is the last thing on my mind and my foot begins to bounce like a jackhammer. I pry my attention away from Jasmine and start flipping through the chapter.

I want to have everything stop dead—to stay huddled with Jasmine over that textbook forever. Even though we're slogging through a calculus problem, one of those ones about water flowing out of a funnel, my heart is pounding and I can feel the heat blasting from my collar.

"Who the hell figured all this stuff out?" Jasmine asks.

"Related rates?"

"All this stuff. It's so hard."

"Dead guys. Isaac Newton did a lot of it. Kind of cool, though. It's one thing to do the math. Once you know how, you just plug in the numbers. But to figure it out in the first place, that's genius."

Jasmine's eyes smile at me.

"What?" I say.

"It's cute how you get all into this math stuff."

My face gets hot all over again and all I want to do is kiss her. The need pounds in my chest. I look at Jasmine's dark, red lips and wonder what she would do if I leaned over and did it. Would she kiss me back? Would she slap me? Would she tell Jim?

The bell over the door jingles and Scott rushes in. A gust of wind whips into the store and bites at my forearms. "Jesus, it's cold out there," he says. "Once that sun goes down it gets like that ice planet in *Empire Strikes Back*."

And there it goes. The moment, if there was one at all, is gone, whisked straight out the door with all the heat. I was dancing a perfect waltz with the girl of my dreams, and halfway through the song someone whipped out a machine gun and filled the band with lead. And I got hit with a few stray bullets.

"We're still playing Four Horsemen tonight, right?" Scott asks.

I shrug and nod, hoping Jasmine might not notice.

"Great," Scott says. "See you about eight. I'll order the pizza." And as quick as he ruined everything, Scott disappears.

I pull out one of the last nylon bags and go back to tagging.

D E A D   M A N ' S   H A N D

(an ace and an eight)

So I figured out what I want to do with my life," Scott tells me across the table. The ancient speakers in the living room send a tinny-sounding Doors song into the kitchen from Scott's father's old record player. Scott draws the top card from the deck and plays a Zombie Hoard card.

"This isn't going to be one of those get-rich-quick pyramid schemes you've been babbling about, is it?"

"Nah, I found out they were illegal."

I counter Scott's move with an Exorcism card. It puts his zombies out of play and allows me to draw two extra cards. "Let me guess—you want to be a cult leader."

Scott ponders that as he gulps down the dregs of his Coke. "Nah," he says. "I don't want to get killed in an FBI raid. Plus, poisoned Kool-Aid isn't my thing."

My turn. I draw a card from the pile and lay down a Maniac Monkeys. The deck has only four cards that can defend against it. Two are already in the discard pile, and I'm holding the other two in my hand. Maniac Monkeys also gives me an extra turn.

Four Horsemen is a pretty straightforward game. It's more colorful, but not much more sophisticated than War, Go Fish, or Uno. We played Four Horsemen continuously the summer after seventh grade, when Scott's parents were getting divorced. Since then, it's been "our game." That is, it was until last year, when I saw a poker tournament on cable. I instantly fell in love with Texas Hold 'Em. The rules and betting structure allow so much more room for creativity. Scott clings to Four Horsemen like it's a life raft, though. It helped get him through the divorce, which was pretty messy, with all sorts of screaming and throwing stuff out onto the lawn. "Three points of damage," I say. "So what've you decided to do with your life?"

Scott marks the damage on his scorecard. "I want to open a strip club."

"What do you know about strip clubs? You've never even been."

"What's there to know? Naked chicks and beer—it's a winning combination." A grin creeps across Scott's face. "I have a name picked out, too."

"I'm sure you do."

Scott holds out his hands and stares into space as though he can already see the neon sign. "Peek-a-Boob," he says.

"I think you might have trouble getting approval from the zoning board."

"Why? *Boob*'s not a bad word."

"You sound just like Rooster, and he's five."

"Great minds think alike." Scott refills his Coke, crams an Oreo Double Stuf into his mouth, and makes his way back to the table. "The other name I'm thinking about—this one's great. Hang on a second." He darts into the living room. The Doors cuts off in the middle of "Five to One," and I hear Scott fumbling through the album collection. Finally, the needle finds its place and folk music drifts into the kitchen. Just a single guitar and some guy with a twangy sort of voice.

"What is this crap?" I call.

Scott comes back into the kitchen. His pointer fingers make little U's in the air like he's conducting an orchestra. "I found it in my dad's record collection. It's a song from the sixties."

"What's this got to do with a strip club?"

"The song is called 'Alice's Restaurant,' " Scott says. "I would name my strip club Alice's *Breastaurant*." As if on cue, the chorus kicks in, and Scott sings along with his own lyrics:

"You can get anything you want at Alice's
     Breastaurant.
The chicks in here are really hot at Alice's
     Breastaurant.
Walk right in it's around the back.
Just have a beer and look at some rack.
You can get anything you want at Alice's
     Breastaurant."

"You've got a lot of problems," I say and fan my cards.

"It's perfect!" Scott howls.

I pop open the freezer and grab a Snickers bar. "While you're at it, why don't you open a pornography store and call it the *Pubic* Library?"

"That's a good one," Scott says. He scribbles it in the margin of his scorecard. "Maybe I'll use it."

I clench down on the frozen candy and work my teeth through the rock-hard caramel. Just when my jaw feels like it's going to break, a hunk of Snickers splinters off and melts in my mouth.

"So, you in Jasmine's pants yet?" Scott asks.

"What?"

"Forget the poker-face crap with me. It's totally obvious you like her."

"I do not," I say. I hide behind my cards and play a Gemstone Dragon. "How're you gonna counter that one?"

Scott places a Force Cage card on my dragon. "I don't know," he says, "but now I have three turns to figure it out."

"Where'd you get a Force Cage?"

"I got it in a booster pack a few weeks ago." Scott draws a card from the stack and adds it to his hand. "It's okay, you liking Jasmine. She's hot." Scott grins—practically drools—like he's about to dig in to a huge steak. "She can have a job at my strip club any time."

"Shut up, asshole."

"See, I knew you have the hots for her. But like I said, I approve."

"Well, I'm glad." And actually, I am. It's the first time the idea of wanting someone to approve of me liking Jasmine crosses my mind, but something about it feels good. I wonder what my parents would think. I'm sure my father would freak out. He likes Jasmine as an employee because she's reliable, but he had trouble hiring her in the first place because of the Goth thing—all the earrings, dark clothes, and makeup. He thought she would scare away the customers. The first time he saw her tongue barbell, he nearly fired her. I couldn't imagine him wanting her at the Thanksgiving table. Mom probably wouldn't say anything if I went out with

Jasmine, but she might not step in if my father flipped out.

"So have you made a move yet?" Scott asks.

"Nah," I say. "It'd be weird. What if she doesn't like me back? I'd still have to work with her every day. And then there's her boyfriend, Jim—"

"Gimme a break," Scott cuts in. "Just say something. You know, something flirty but low-key so it won't be so bad when she turns you down—if she turns you down."

"Oh, great, so you expect she'll turn me down."

"Shut up and listen. I was watching some talk show a few weeks ago. They had a thing on about dating in the workplace. They said it can be good for the business, not that you really care about that. But the lady—I think she was a psychologist or something—said the best way to do it is to ask the person you like to lunch. You know, something low-key like that. Then if nothing happens, there won't be any awkward stuff later on."

"We get there at three. We don't have lunch."

"That's just an example. Think of something else. You guys were doing homework today. It's the dorkiest thing in the world, but why don't you ask her to the library?"

"I was helping her with calculus."

"Perfect. Offer to tutor her. It's stupid to be head over heels for her and—"

"I'm not head over heels."

"Whatever, it's stupid for you to be 'interested' in her and just hang around like some kind of martyr. It's a waste to be alone together for so many hours every week and not take advantage of the big, soft piles of laundry in the back."

"Dude, it's other people's dirty clothes."

"Come on, tell me the thought hasn't crossed your mind."

"Nasty," I say.

"Yeah, bullshit. You've thought about it."

Scott's relaxed attitude around girls—and how casual he is talking about sex—blows my mind. As for me, I can't seem to get down the right arm of my algorithm. I drew it in trigonometry class last year in the hope I could figure this whole thing out. I can still see it in my head:

GUY MEETS GIRL ALGORITHM

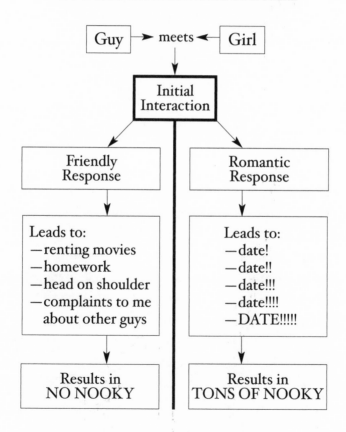

The thick line down the center was to remind me that once a guy passed the Initial Interaction Phase, there was no hopping left or right. Something happened at that moment to irrevocably cast him one way or the other.

And I always went to the left.

I swore to one day create an algorithm of the Initial Interaction Phase—to break it down into even smaller steps—so I could figure out what I'm doing wrong. The solution still eludes me.

Even when I get that vibe from a girl—the vibe that tells me she might be interested—I'm afraid if I make a move and she doesn't like me back I'd feel like a total idiot. Worse than an idiot. I'd feel totally humiliated, like every kid at school would point and laugh at me as I walked down the hall. I'd never leave the house again.

"Anyhow," Scott continues, "you'd better make a move soon. Remember what happened in sixth grade at Kimberly Kellogg's birthday party."

He had to bring it up. Hell, he always brings it up. When I was in sixth grade, I got shoved into a closet with Jodi Lemmer for that cruelest of games, Five Minutes in Heaven. After about two minutes of my dodging her lips, she managed to pin me against the vacuum cleaner. Then she planted a kiss on my ear as I thrashed side to side. I pushed Jodi off me, and she began to cry. We just sat there for the remaining three minutes of hell. I had to listen to her sob "What's wrong with me?" over and over, until finally the other kids let us out. Then she told everyone I was gay.

It's not like Scott's gotten any further around the bases than me, but when he's talking to girls he's totally at ease.

Maybe Scott's used to girls because of his sister back in Cincinnati; maybe it's because he's just so goofy. Either way, Scott has a knack for disarming them—getting them to feel comfortable around him. At school, he has his own little female fan club. It's kind of a nerdy fan club, mostly marching band and flag team girls, but it's a fan club nonetheless.

The doorbell rings, and Scott catapults from his seat. "Pizza," he says. Then he hollers at the front door, "Be right there!" He disappears into his father's room. I hear a drawer slide open. He comes out with several bills in his hand and heads to the front.

Moments later, he returns to the kitchen with two pizza boxes in his arms. "One's got extra cheese and pepperoni," he says. "The other's mushrooms and onions." He drops the boxes on the table, knocking the deck and the scorecards to the floor.

"Hey, the game—"

"Screw the game," Scott says. "You were kicking my ass anyway."

I open one of the pizza boxes, and the steam blasts me in the face. "It's wild," I say. "My father would never leave money in a drawer and let me take it whenever I wanted."

"My dad's always away on business," Scott says. "That or he's at his girlfriend's house. I have to buy food and stuff on my own all the time. Anyhow, since the divorce, he wants to keep me happy so I don't go running back to Mom's. As long as I don't take too much, he doesn't say anything."

"That's awesome," I say. "How much is too much?"

"I don't know. Depends on his mood or if he's afraid the company he works at is going to cut back. One time I bought some CDs, a bunch of booster packs, and a few rare single cards, and he freaked out. Between that and food and a pair of pants I needed, I guess it was a little over two hundred bucks in a week."

"Man, you've got it made."

"It's not so great," he says. "He's never here. I don't even know why my dad wants me to live with him so bad. It's like I'm some kind of trophy or something—like he got one over on my mom by getting custody of me."

"Well, I'd take no dad over my father any day."

Scott only shrugs.

I pull two pepperoni slices from the box and scrape the cheese stuck to the lid onto my plate. I top off my soda and go into the living room. The living room is my favorite spot in Scott's house. Sitting in one of the unmatched La-Z-Boys feels like wearing an old sweater. A lumpy couch sits against the opposite wall. All the seats angle toward the big-screen television, which sits precariously on a veneered entertainment center. Stacks of old newspapers and magazines fill the fireplace beyond capacity, and two massive bookcases are crowded with all sorts of books, from world history to quantum physics.

I settle into one of the recliners, and Scott sits on the other. He hits the remote and MTV comes on. Tricked-out cars bounce on their hydraulics to the beat, and women in short shorts shake their butts at the camera.

"Good educational programming," Scott says. He turns down the volume but leaves the video on. "So, how's the poker career going? Taking them all to the cleaners?"

"Ha, ha," I say through my half-chewed mouthful. "I've been having a run of bad cards."

"How bad?"

"Very. I took a bad beat on a full house. The guy pulled a four-of-a-kind out of his ass on the flop."

"What's the flop?"

"The first group of cards shown. It was less than a one-percent chance."

"Ouch."

"Ouch is right."

"So, how bad is bad?"

"I'm about six hundred in the hole." Somehow saying "six hundred" instead of "six hundred *dollars*" makes it seem like less of a loss.

"Whose hole? Some kind of bookie or loan shark? That fat, creepy guy who runs the poker club or something? What'd you tell me his name was? Sushi?"

"Shushie. But, no. You watch too many movies."

"Then who?"

"No one."

"Bullshit. Unless they're giving out credit cards to high school kids, you can't be 'in the hole' unless it's someone else's hole."

I take a bite of pizza to delay the inevitable a few chews longer. *How will Scott take it? He's got a weird sense of morals. Sometimes he gets all Sir Lancelot on me.* I gulp down some soda to cool the fire behind my face. "My father," I finally say.

"Your father lends you money to play poker?"

"Not exactly."

It takes a few seconds for the weight of my words to sink in. When they do, Scott leans forward and fixes his eyes on mine. "You're stealing from the dry cleaners?"

"Borrowing."

"Does your father know you're borrowing?"

I shift my gaze to the television.

"If he doesn't know about it," Scott says, "you're stealing. And if you're stealing to play poker, that's a major problemo. My dad told me my uncle lost his house shooting dice and—"

"Jesus, I'm not a gambler!" I say it like he told me I have a second head growing out of my shoulder. "I just had a run of bad cards."

"I wish I had a tape recorder so you could listen to your-self—"

"Lay off. Poker's a game of skill. It's not the luck of the draw, like blackjack or those other casino games. I'm playing against the other people at the table. As long as I'm better than a few of them, I'll make money. People make their living playing poker."

"So that's what you want to do with your life? You want to be a professional poker player?"

"Maybe. Like I said, over time I win. It's all numbers. Poker is about knowing the odds, and that's what I'm good at. It's what I've always been good at."

"Obviously you're not good enough. You should stick with Four Horsemen. You won't lose money that way."

"Screw Four Horsemen," I say. "That game is for dorks."

Scott's leg starts pumping up and down, and it sets his La-Z-Boy rocking. "At least I'm not losing my father's money playing it, asshole. Anyhow, you wanna talk about a dork, you're the one who can't even talk to a freaking girl."

The pizza leaves my hand before I realize what I'm do-ing—like someone else is pulling the strings to make me hurl my dinner at my friend. With the reflexes of a housefly, Scott flings himself back into the La-Z-Boy, and the pizza sails past him. It splatters against the wall and sticks there. Scott's mo-mentum causes the leg rest of the recliner to fire out, and the whole chair topples backward. Scott lands against the stereo and cracks his head on the corner of the floor speaker. The pizza slowly slides to the floor, leaving a vertical stripe of tomato sauce and oil on the pale green paint.

"Oh, God, I'm sorry, Scott," I say. I scramble to help him up, but he shoves me away.

"Get the hell off me!" He leaps to his feet.

I spin around and start wiping at the stain on the wall with my paper towel. "I'm sorry. I'll clean everything up."

As I frantically dab, I realize Scott isn't making a sound. I turn around. He's standing beside the toppled recliner with his fists balled up. He's clenching his jaw so tightly that it looks like he's trying to crush a golf ball between his molars. A thin trickle of blood makes its way from behind his ear to the collar of his T-shirt. "Get out," he utters.

"Scott, you're bleeding—"

"Get out!"

"Whatever," I mutter and push past him to the kitchen. I grab my coat from the chair and fling open the side door. Glancing back through the archway to the living room, I be-gin to open my mouth.

"Get out of my house!" he screams.

I enter the night. Scott's neighbor, Mrs. Foster, pokes her head out between her drapes and stares at me. I pretend not to notice her, focusing instead on how the porch light catches my breath in the air. It looks as thick as a ghost. It's freezing out, but I'm still sweating. I swing a leg over my bike and begin to pedal—faster and faster—until my lungs are filled with broken glass.

I don't need him.

Four Horsemen is for fairies.

That jackass is still stuck in seventh grade.

He's the one who needs to grow up.

Insult after insult rattles through my brain until I'm convinced that I was right. My mind races faster than my legs until I find myself pedaling up my driveway. I hop off the bike while it's still moving, and let it crash into the garbage cans. I wriggle my key into the front door and go inside. My mom keeps this place so damn hot. I yank off my jacket and make for the stairs. My father says something to me over the din of the television, but his words don't penetrate my fury.

The slam of my bedroom door is the first thing that gives me any relief.

"Honey, are you okay?" My mother's voice barely reaches me through my door.

"Fine."

Her head pokes in, and all I want is for her to get out. "Would you like to talk about it?"

"No. I'm just gonna check my e-mail and go to sleep."

"All right. I'll be downstairs reading if you change your mind."

"Night."

I boot up my computer. My instant messaging program kicks on automatically, and I see that Scott is online, too. Almost reflexively, my cursor moves across the screen to open a chat window with him. Then I stop, shut the program, and click the online poker icon.

Now it's *my* leg pumping furiously.

Over the next few hours, I play aggressively. I increase my play-money winnings from $250,525 to $365,950. The other online players are particularly chatty, but I remain silent. Immersing myself in the numbers settles me down some, until somewhere around four o'clock, I crawl into bed. Even though I'm totally wiped out, I stare at the ceiling for the next three hours, until my alarm goes off.

DIMES
(two tens)

Mrs. Nussbaum," I say, sliding her balled-up black crepe dress across the counter to her. "Like I told you, we don't turn on our pressing machines on the weekend."

"I have a formal affair tonight—my nephew's bar mitzvah reception," she says in a raspy smoker's voice. "It's at the Regal Crystal Manor," she adds, like that tidbit should get my knees knocking. Mrs. Nussbaum looks down her nose at her fingers like she's thinking whoever did her manicure should get the ax. "I've been a customer here for years now. Your father will do it for me."

"We can't. It takes forty-five minutes to get the steam going in the machines, and the pressing guy isn't even here on Saturdays." The words pour from my mouth. I can't keep my mind off Scott and all the crap that happened last night.

"Your father's in the back, isn't he?" Her question filters in through the edges of my sleep-deprived haze. It feels like all the wires in my head are tangled up and any information that comes my way has to be decoded first, then analyzed, then interpreted.

"He's doing paperwork."

"Go ask him," she says as though each word is its own sentence.

I let my head sway on my shoulders like it's about to fall off. My eyes roll up so far I get a headache. I already know what my father is going to say. When we came in this morning, like every Saturday, he specifically told me not to take in any special rush orders. He's going to tell me to make Mrs. Nussbaum take a hike. But I drag my feet to the back anyway. I'll let him deal with it. He's probably sitting on his ass reading the sports page anyway.

Before my grandfather died—when he ran this place—I remember him saying that 10 percent of your customers give you 90 percent of your headaches. Well, Mrs. Nussbaum is a major headache. Nothing is ever simple with her. She always wants everyone else to go that extra mile—press something right away, put the stain stickers on every little spot, carry stuff to her car, or whatever. And who the hell wears a dusty rose sweat suit with patches of black pleather and sequins sewn all over it, anyway?

"Hey," I say to my father.

"Hey there, son of mine."

His eyes are riveted to the television. It's an old fourteen-inch black-and-white number that was probably built before Abe Lincoln was born. My father is catching the sports segment of the local news. His feet are up on the desk, where a bunch of basketball pool sheets, unpaid bills, and old dry-cleaning tickets lie scattered. A pint of leftover Chinese food is resting on his gut. "Those goddamn River Rats," he says. "They can't win a game." My father looks up at me. "Want some?" He offers me the Manchurian beef. His chopsticks are sticking out of the top like two bug antennae. A dark rectangle of grease stains his sweatshirt where the box of stir-fry was.

"No thanks," I say. It's not that I don't like Manchurian beef. Actually, it's one of my favorites—sweet, fried, and no vegetables. I just can't stand the idea of someone else's used, wet, nasty chopsticks—especially my father's—in my mouth. And Chinese food at ten in the morning is kind of gross anyway.

I flip my thumb toward the front of the store. "Mrs. Nussbaum wants you."

My father looks up at me again. "You look like shit," he says, like I should give him a medal for his honest opinion.

"I didn't get a lot of sleep last night."

He nods and sticks a piece of meat in his mouth. "What's Mrs. Nussbaum want?"

"She wants something pressed—a dress."

"Tell her no," he says.

"I did. She told me to check with you."

"Tell her Jules isn't here." He slaps the television on the side, and the snowy image jiggles up and down. It ends up worse than before.

"I did that already. I also told her how the machines take forty-five minutes to warm up. She told me to check with you."

"What would you do if I wasn't here?" my father says. He puts the Chinese food container down on the desk. "How can I trust you to watch this place if you can't handle a simple customer?"

"Mrs. Nussbaum is no simple customer," I say. "She's a demon who wears rhinestones."

This puts a little smile on my father's face, but it doesn't last long. "You're going to inherit this place someday. You have to learn how to be a manager—an owner. You can't just run back here every time something gets tough."

All I can think of is how much I *don't* want this place. It would suck to make dry cleaning my career. Getting up well before sunrise. Dealing with other people's soiled clothes all day. Doing the same thing every day for my whole life until I keeled over at an early age from sucking in all those chemicals for so many years. I can just see my headstone:

ANDREW LANG

1991–2042

HE MAY HAVE DIED EARLY

BUT DANG OUR CLOTHES WERE CLEAN

Totally depressing. I'd probably sell this place—maybe to those Korean guys who were talking to my dad a few months back. But I'd never tell my father that. This place has been in my family for a long time.

As he pushes himself up out of his seat, my father looks at me with those eyes that tell me he thinks I'm totally incompetent. He squeezes past me because I'm standing right in the opening of his alcove. I don't step aside because somehow staying put makes me feel in control—like I made him move for once, not the other way around.

I trail behind him to the front. My father walks on his toes and steps down real heavy every time he plants his foot. From years of walking like that and being as heavy as he is, his calves are huge. They look like two footballs glued to the backs of his legs. I can see them through his sweatpants. I look down at my own legs to make sure I don't do the same thing when I walk.

I don't.

At least I don't think I do.

My father plods to the front counter. I stop at the tagging station, the one Jasmine usually stands at. I dump out one of the nylon bags. It's weird because I can still smell that fruity smell she was wearing yesterday.

"Hi, Joyce," my father says.

"Oh, Howie, thank God you're here. Your son told me I couldn't get something pressed today. I need this dress for Jeremy's bar mitzvah tonight. You can do it, right?"

My father gives a single nod and reaches behind the pressing machine. The pipes start clanging and knocking as the steam begins to build up pressure.

"We don't usually turn on the machines on Saturday, Joyce, but for you . . ." He taps the pressure gauge with his fingertip to make sure the needle isn't stuck.

"Thanks, sweetheart," Mrs. Nussbaum says. Then she starts sucking air through her back molars like she's trying to dislodge a pork chop that got stuck back there.

My father glances at the clock over the pay phone. "Why don't you come back at one, Joyce? We'll have it done by then." My father will also be long gone by then. I'll be the one dealing with her.

He grabs the dress from the counter and spreads it across the padded surface of the pressing machine. The dress looks like one of those Thanksgiving parade balloons on the street before they blow it up—all flat and shapeless. Then my father looks at me. "No charge, Andrew."

I glance up from stapling and nod. My face is already hotter than the steam pipes.

Mrs. Nussbaum purses her lips. Between her wrinkles and her too-dark lipstick, her mouth looks like a blood clot. She shoots me one of those I-told-you-so expressions and says, "Thanks, Howie. See you at one." Then she walks out like she's holding a loaf of bread between her ass cheeks. Everything about her makes me sick.

"You know, Andrew, you have to learn to handle these things. Now I'll be late for the JV game."

I fire a staple into Detective Scotti's pants, right through the fabric and everything. "I'll do it. I'm gonna be here anyway."

"If it was anything else I'd say okay, but crepe is too delicate."

"What's the big deal? I've seen Jules do it a thousand times. I'll just put the steam on the lightest setting and blow it out on the mannequin. Too bad we don't have a fatter mannequin though."

My father smirks at that and trots to the register. As he opens the drawer, everything starts churning inside me. It's not like I grabbed any more money this morning, but it's been slow today, and that always gets him riled up. "What's going on?" he says, more to the cash drawer than to me.

"Huh?" I say.

"Why's it been so slow lately? Isn't anyone picking up their clothes?"

It has been slow, but I have to play it down. "It's seemed busy to me these past few weeks. Tuesday we were jamming."

"Receipts have been off." He opens the black binder he keeps under the register. "We're a few thousand dollars below our usual December deposits and way behind last month."

"Maybe it's that new dry cleaners out on the highway by Shu— out by that pool hall." Jesus, I almost slipped. Stupid, stupid, stupid. "Maybe we're losing business to them."

"Not this much." He pushes his fingers through his hair. "It's never been this bad." My father and I go through this conversation just about every other week. He complains about how slow it's been and I reassure him that it's not as bad as he thinks.

"Just get out of here and let me handle things," I say. I just want him to start thinking about basketball instead of the cash register. "Who's the JV team playing anyhow?"

"The Pine Mountain Lumberjacks."

"Shouldn't they be called the Lumber*jills*?" I dump another bag of clothing on the counter. Mr. Miller's stuff. He drops off and picks up every Friday, rotating five shirts, a few suits, and some miscellaneous articles every week. Mr. Miller works down in New York City during the week, and he comes in like clockwork.

"I suppose it *should* be the Lumberjills," my father says. "Never thought about it before." He snaps the black binder shut, shoves it under the counter, and heads to the back. I let out the hot, stale air I've been holding in the deepest parts of my lungs.

Crisis averted.

A weird song from the fifties comes on the radio. Some

guy with a girlie kind of voice crackles through the speakers, howling about a sleeping lion. I can't believe that song was ever popular.

I fire the tags into the clothes and check the pockets with lightning speed. With all the sweeping I've been blowing off and all the tagging and bagging that still need to be done, there's no doubt I'll be here past three, not that I have anything else to do today. Maybe I'll catch up on some homework later on or—even better—some sleep.

My hands move like hyperactive spiders. Not a movement is wasted. It's weird how I can get so focused on stupid tasks like tagging clothes. My mind goes someplace else and I can tag all day like a robot. Sometimes I think I'd be better off working in a factory—on an assembly line or something—than going to college and getting some office job like my mom wants. That way, I could be happy with my benefits and complaining about my boss all the time instead of having to think about every little thing.

It's one of the reasons I tend to do so well playing poker. Don't get me wrong, there's a lot of thinking that goes on in poker, but I have the patience to wait for the good starting hands to come along, not to jump in because playable cards haven't come my way in a while. The worst thing someone can do is to go "on tilt"—which means they're betting stupid because they get frustrated. I pride myself on never allowing myself to do that. Never.

My hand slides into the inside pocket of Mr. Miller's overcoat. When I was Rooster's age, I used to call that pocket the secret agent pocket. I always pictured secret agents carrying their guns or bundles of classified documents in there. I kept asking my mom for a jacket with an inside pocket until she got me a sportcoat for my cousin's wedding. It was like a straightjacket around my shoulders. And the tie practically choked me to death. After that, I never asked her for clothes again.

Anyhow, I used to forget to check the inside pocket all the time until I missed three ballpoint pens in one week. They burst all over the clothing in the dry-cleaning machine and ruined everything. My dad had to put in a claim to the insurance company for those disasters. He still brings it up every now and then, when he runs out of other stuff to harp on me about. Now, I never miss the inside pocket.

I feel something plastic. It feels lumpy, too, like a Baggie filled with sand. I pull whatever it is out and drop it on the counter in case it's something nasty. But as soon as I see it, I know what it is. The word blares across my mind. *Drugs.* A zipper-lock sandwich bag sits there on the counter filled halfway with little, white, gravelly bits. I don't know what kind because I don't know the first thing about drugs. Maybe crack, I guess.

I hear my dad's heavy footsteps behind me. I pull Mr. Miller's clothes over the Baggie and turn to see my father working his arm into the sleeve of his jacket.

"Need anything?" he says. "I'm gonna blow out of here."

"Nuh-uh" is all I can get out. That, and a too-rapid shake of my head.

"Everything okay?"

"Fine," I manage. "Everything's fine."

"Good." His answer sends my blood pressure from life-threatening down to way too high. "I'm headed over to the school. If you need me, get me on my cell." He pats his hip where he always keeps it.

"Sure." I turn all the way around and lean against the tagging station so I can hide the clothes on the counter with my body. Even though it sounds weird, keeping myself between him and the drugs calms me some.

"You sure everything's okay?"

"Yeah," I say. I wiggle my hand around. "I just nipped my finger with the stapler. I'll get a Band-Aid from the back after you go."

"All right." He turns to leave but then keeps wobbling on his axis until he's facing me again. "Oh, by the way, we're going to do a full inventory on Monday. We have to clear out the old orders and get some cash flow in this place. I'll tell your mother we'll be here late. We'll order Chinese."

"Cool."

Two seconds later, the back door slams and he's gone.

Shit. That means I have to get that money back in the drawer or my interest-free loan is going to surface. How am I going to get six hundred dollars by Monday? My blood pressure goes back to life-threatening, and I can feel my heart pulsing all the way to my teeth.

SNOWMEN

(two eights)

I dust off my shoulders and stomp my boots on the cow-shaped doormat in the vestibule of the diner. The snow started only a few minutes ago, but the flakes are the size of dinner plates. Good thing I decided to walk. My bike would've been slipping all over the place.

The smell of grease and burnt coffee reminds me of how my father used to take me here back when I was Rooster's age. The Moocow Diner hasn't changed a bit. It's decorated with nothing but cows from floor to ceiling—cow posters, cow place mats, and cow print aprons. Even the creamers have plastic cow heads on top. When I was little, I thought that was cool, but now the thought of cows puking milk sort of grosses me out.

I sit at the counter, the same stool I always used to sit at, and look for Mandy. Mandy who won the poker tournament a few nights ago. She's serving a bunch of burgers on the other side of a low divider that separates the counter stools from the dining room. She meets my gaze with tired eyes and, once she recognizes me, smiles.

"What can I get for you, hon?" a husky woman's voice asks. The other waitress snuck up on me, her black sneakers silent on the tile. Her name tag says Helen, but the Helen I remember from years ago was about two hundred pounds thinner. The cow print apron doesn't flatter her.

"I'm waiting for Mandy." I flip my thumb toward the dining room. "I don't need anything, thanks."

"If you're going to take the seat, you're going to have to order something," she says like she's reading it from a script. Then her face screws up sort of funny. "Hey, you're Howie Lang's kid, aren't ya?"

I nod.

"For Christmas sake, how's your dad doing? I haven't seen him in ages. You for longer! Andrew, right?"

I nod again.

"Sheesh, you've gotten huge. I barely recognized you. You always ordered the same thing—a strawberry milk shake and a big cookie."

I can't keep my eyes off her teeth, which have all kinds of metal everywhere. Not braces, though. Weird wires run across the roof of her mouth and along her gum line. It's the kind of work someone gets after years of neglect, when the dentist finally has to go in there with a ball-peen hammer and some rebar. Her dental work makes any word with an *s* in it sound like a leaky steam valve.

"I suppose you don't want a milk shake today with all that snow. How about a coffee or a hot chocolate? Something to warm you up."

"Sure," I say. "I'll have a hot chocolate and a big cookie."

"We have chocolate chip, sugar, and black-and-white. We also have some great Linzer tortes straight from Lombardi's Bakery." I almost crack up at how she says "Linzer tortes" and consider asking her to repeat my options.

"Sugar," I say.

"Plain, chocolate sprinkles, or rainbow?"

Jesus. I hate all these damn questions. Every time I answer one she comes back at me with another.

I shrug. "Rainbow, I guess."

"Does Mandy know you want to see her?"

"I doubt it."

"I'll let her know," she says with her bear trap smile.

She walks away, and I start playing with the cow creamer. The plastic is so faded I can barely see the cow's blue eyes. It's probably the same one I horsed around with when I was a kid.

"I'll never forget. It was years ago. You couldn't have been more than five," Helen says as she puts down the hot chocolate and the cookie. Damn, those shoes are quiet. "You were playing with one of them creamers and you looked up to your dad and asked him that question. You remember the question I'm talking about?"

"Nope." I snap off a piece of the cookie. It's really crumbly and dry. It always looks better in the case than it really is, and all of a sudden I don't want to eat the cookie anymore. I don't want to talk with Helen, either.

"Oh, we laughed about it for days around here. Louie, God rest his soul, he was gonna get it typed up real nice and put it in a frame. He never got around to it, though."

"What'd I say?"

"You were playing with one of them moo-cow creamers and turned to him all serious and said, 'Hey, Dad, when cows laugh really hard does milk come out their nose?' Lou was bringing a case of eggs up from the cooler. He nearly dropped them right where I'm standing. I'm surprised milk didn't come out of *his* nose. We talked about it for days."

They must not have had much to talk about, I figure.

Helen takes the creamer and slides it back with the ketchup and salt and pepper shakers, almost as though she's afraid I'm going to spill it. "Anyhow, enjoy. Mandy'll be over as soon as she gets a chance. Take off your coat and stay awhile."

With a Baggie full of drugs in my pocket, I wouldn't take my jacket off if it were ninety-nine degrees with 110 percent humidity in here.

I have a few more bites of the cookie and try to figure out what I'm going to say to Mandy. The hot chocolate is good. They probably make it with milk instead of water. But there's no way I could possibly enjoy it. I let my hand slide into my coat pocket and feel the Baggie. It's much lighter than I would expect a bag of such terrible stuff to be.

"Hey."

I jump and look up. It's Mandy.

"Hey," I say. "Congratulations on the tournament. I heard you cleaned up."

"Tournaments come and go," she says quietly. Her eyes are sunk deep in their sockets, like she hasn't slept in days. "I've lost a lot more of them than I've won. It was just the only action around." She leans on the counter on her elbows. She'd be kind of pretty if she didn't look so washed out.

"I have a question for you," I say.

"Well, I figure you didn't come down here for the cookie." She slides my plate away and dumps the rainbow sprinkle sugar cookie into the garbage can behind the counter. It lands with a heavy thud. I'm surprised it doesn't put a hole in the floor. "Should've had the Linzer torte," she says.

"Hey, is there anywhere we could talk?"

Mandy jerks her head toward the door. "I need a cigarette anyway. Let's go." She grabs her coat, and I drop a five on the counter. We head outside. It's only around three-thirty, but it's already getting dark. We walk around the side of the building. The streetlight is on, and it makes the falling snow look like millions of cotton balls.

"Damn smoking laws," Mandy says. "It's cold out here." She fumbles with her cigarette and lights up. "What'cha want?" She exhales a lungful of smoke, sending it tumbling into the air. As soon as the smoke leaves the radius of the streetlight, it disappears into the darkness like it was never there.

"I'm sure you've noticed I had a few bad beats these past couple of weeks—"

"I knew it," she says. "Look, just because I won that tournament, don't come looking to me for money. I have my own problems." Snowflakes land on her eyelashes and make her look about a hundred years old.

"I'm just a little in the hole and—"

"We're all in the hole," she says. Her arms are wrapped around her body like she's holding herself up, like she'd fall right down otherwise. The only time she lets go of herself is to hoist the cigarette to her lips. "If you want to spend your life playing cards, you'd better get used to looking at everything from the bottom of a goddamn hole."

"Look, I'm not begging here. I was talking to Shush and—"

"And what? What'd Shushie tell you?"

"Nothing, just . . ." I pull the Baggie from my pocket and hold it palm up but tight against my body so no one from the parking lot can see.

"Where'd you get that?" she says. She steps in closer, and I know I have her attention.

"It doesn't matter. I need some seed money and thought you might be interested."

"Shushie tell you that?" she snaps. "Shushie tell you I might be interested?"

"No," I say. "He never said anything like that. I just got my hands on it and I thought . . ."

"Jesus, there's a shitload there. How much is that?" She moves in even closer like she might be able to inhale the whole Baggie. I can smell the cigarette smoke on her breath, and I take a small step back.

"There's around a hundred and twenty-five of those little pieces," I say. "The biggest ones are about the size of a small pearl."

It's true. I counted them before I locked up the cleaners. I made a pile of them on the Formica and pushed them back into the bag with a ballpoint pen like I've seen the pharmacist do when I pick up my mom's migraine medicine. I didn't want to touch the stuff with my fingers because I was afraid it could get in my pores or something.

"Rocks," she says.

"Rocks? It's crack, then?"

"You don't even know what it is?" she says. "You're walking around with close to four grand in crack and you don't even know what you're carrying around?"

"I'm not a drug dealer or anything. I just came across it and—"

"Shushie put you up to this, didn't he?"

"No," I say. "I just came across it and—"

"Get the fuck out of here," Mandy says, trembling. She lifts her cigarette to her mouth and takes a last drag. She drops it to the ground and grinds the butt out with her toe, leaving a small circle of melted snow through which I can see the blacktop.

"You tell Shushie he can fuck off. Tell him to stop fucking with me." Her hands are shaking even more now, and I move closer because I think she might topple right over. "I'm off that shit. Get away from me." She takes a bunch of steps back and almost falls right into a snow-covered bush.

I lunge forward to catch her arm, but that gets her to start scrambling more frantically. I never expected Mandy to react like this. I back away from her. All of a sudden I think she might scream for the police, so I jam the Baggie back into my pocket and take off.

I run until the icy air gnaws at the insides of my lungs, begging me to stop. I ignore the pain until I hear a voice calling my name over and over and it's all I can do just to turn around.

SPEED LIMIT
(two fives)

Andrew!" The voice floats to me through the wall of snowflakes several times before I recognize it. My chest feels like a fiery bellows. I bend forward and put my hands on my knees to catch my breath.

"Jesus," Jasmine says. "Are you okay?" Her face is paler than I've ever seen it, and she has on even more dark lipstick and eyeliner than usual. Against the near whiteout, she looks ominous, but the sight of her makes me warm in a weird sort of way.

I nod a bunch of times because I can't get any words out.

"I was coming out of the coffeehouse and you tore right past me."

I gulp, but my throat is lined with sandpaper.

"You sure you're okay?" She comes closer and puts a hand on my shoulder. It makes me even warmer. "It looks like you've been crying."

"No," I pant. "Just the . . . cold . . . in my eyes."

"What're you running in a snowstorm for? Are you trying out for your dad's team or something?"

I manage a "Yeah, right," and go back to panting.

"I will not wait until Monday to hear this one." She grabs

the sleeve of my jacket and leads me to the coffeehouse like I'm a lost little boy at the supermarket.

Her black wool peacoat is buttoned to the top. I've always wanted one of those—maybe in navy blue—but I was afraid it might be too girlie looking. Looks great on her, though.

Despite the dorky name, Light and Sweet Café is a pretty cool place. Every once in a while Scott and I study here, mostly when the college kids have exams and the library is packed like a refugee camp. The café has a bunch of small tables and a boatload of those wicker chairs with the high, round backs that Morticia Addams sits in. They play some pretty cool music, too—jazz, fusion, and acoustic stuff mostly. Some Christmas song is playing now. But the best part is that you can sit here all day and nurse a cup of coffee or a hot chocolate. The owner never pesters you to buy anything else.

Jasmine sits in one of the big wicker chairs. It frames her perfectly. She looks like a snow queen or something. She pops the lid off her mocha latte and takes a noisy sip. I order a glass of water for my throat and a cinnamon spice mochaccino. Caffeine settles me down.

"So what was that all about? You were running like the devil herself was on your heels."

"Herself?"

"Who knows? The devil might be a woman."

"Probably is," I mutter. My breathing is mostly under control now. "Guys aren't crafty enough."

Jasmine smiles at that and opens her coat. "Well, I've got some time. I have to hear this."

"What happened with Jim last night at the party?" I ask.

"You don't want to know," she says. "It was pretty ugly."

"You guys break up?"

It's weird. With a pocketful of crack, it's much easier to ask Jasmine about what's going on with Jim. I'm not so concerned about letting on that I'm interested in her. It's like the stakes have been raised and hiding my attraction doesn't matter so much anymore.

She doesn't answer. "Why were you tearing through downtown?" she asks.

I sit in silence, and Jasmine gives me time to gather my words. She's cool like that; she knows when to give a guy some space. Most girls would be all pushy for an answer.

The waitress brings over my glass of water and my mochaccino. I stir the coffee with the little wooden stick until all the whipped cream dissolves.

"I have a little bit of a thing going on," I finally say.

"What sort of thing?"

"A money thing."

"A money thing?"

I nod and drink the whole glass of water in a few huge gulps. The cold liquid knocks my throat from a four-alarm fire to two alarms.

"Look, am I going to have to torture you? Just tell me what's going on already."

"Sorry," I say and look back down at my mochaccino. "It's just hard for me to tell someone."

"Try me. I stopped judging people after my sixth or seventh piercing."

"Where *was* your seventh piercing?"

She smiles. "Wouldn't you like to know?"

Actually I would, but I also know that if I keep on dancing

around the subject it'll piss Jasmine off and then she'll get all irritated and then I'll never have a chance with her. "All right, well . . . I play cards." I say it like it's supposed to be some great revelation, like those three words should unlock some great mystery for her.

"Yeah, I know all about it—that Four Horsies game or whatever it's called."

"It's called Four Horsemen," I say. "But not that."

Jasmine's face rises above the brim of her latte. "Then what? Are you playing Tag-team Tournament Go Fish or something?"

"Poker," I say. "I play Texas Hold 'Em."

She doesn't seem stunned like I thought she would be.

"Yeah?" she says. "So does about every other last person in America. You can't turn on the television without coming across that game. My grandmother plays it with her feeble friends down in Cemetery Village."

"Your grandmother lives in a place called Cemetery Village?"

"Century Village, actually. It's in Florida. But why mince words? It's where the old people go to die."

"Yeah, well, I play for real money, not Sweet'n Low packets like your grandmother. I've been playing for close to a year."

"What do you mean by real money?" Jasmine asks. She leans in a bit.

"You know, real games. Real players. Pots anywhere from fifty or sixty bucks to a few hundred."

"Per hand?"

"Per hand. Some pots get as high as a few thousand, but that's really rare—like when there's someone from out of town playing, someone's drunk off his ass, or some sucker comes in who has no idea what he's doing and he's acting like his money's burning a hole in his pocket."

"How do you afford it?" she asks. "Each hand is like a week's pay—or more."

"I'm good at it," I say. Aside from Scott, no one knows I play poker, so the story bursts out of me like a horse out of the starting gate at Saratoga. "I started playing on the Internet for free. I learned the game there—betting structures, bluffing, and whatnot. Then I found out about the live poker club here in town on a Yahoo message board. I saved my money for a while and took the rest out of my savings account. I started small, and I've been winning consistently for months. I stockpiled close to five grand. The problem is that I've had a run of bad cards and I've burned right through my bankroll."

"So what's the big deal?" Jasmine says. "Just start small again. Wait for your next paycheck."

"I wish it were that simple," I say. I don't want to tell her about the cash I took from the register. Well, I want to. I want to tell her bad, but I know it would be the wrong move. She works at the cleaners, too. Heck, she probably cares more about that place than I do. "Yeah, I guess. I'll just wait until next week."

Jasmine considers me from behind her coffee cup, and I can tell she knows I'm hiding something. I'm positive she's gonna call me on it. Finally, she lowers her cup and says, "That's pretty cool. I was half expecting your story to be something about missing the bus to some Pokémon convention and Pikachu was going to be there signing autographs."

"No one plays Pokémon anymore."

"Well, whatever," Jasmine says. "Anyhow, none of this explains why you were running down the street like a Kenyan marathoner."

"I'm getting to that." My hand moves to my jacket pocket, and I feel the bulge of the Baggie. Part of me wishes it had fallen out when I was running and gotten lost in a snowdrift.

"Well, get to it already," she says. "You're not going anywhere until you tell me, and I have stuff to do this century."

I take a deep breath through my nose to try to purge the jumpy feeling in my chest. It doesn't work, but I start talking anyway. "Mr. Miller, you know, the guy who comes in every Saturday to get his five shirts cleaned?"

"Yeah?" she says, clearly wondering how my story could have anything to do with Mr. Miller. "The guy who works down in the city, right?"

"That's him. He came in like usual. I was checking the pocket of one of his blazers when I found some drugs."

"Wild." Jasmine smiles like she thinks I'm getting all worked up over nothing. "What'd he have, a bunch of joints like we found in Jamie Robinson's winter coat?"

"Not exactly."

"Yeah, I figure Mr. Miller more as a prescription kind of guy," Jasmine says. "Did he have some Percocets or some Vicodins? Maybe some OxyContin? I hear that stuff's supposed to be like heroin." Jasmine's ease around the subject reminds me of how nonchalantly the school nurse talks about sex. Amazing.

I lean in toward her and whisper, "Try a Baggie full of crack."

"Yeah, right."

"I'm serious."

"You probably don't even know what crack looks like."

"Sure I do," I say as though I've known forever. "It looks like little white pebbles."

"You're shitting me. How much of it did he have?"

"A lot. I counted around a hundred and twenty-five rocks."

"Jesus Christ, Andrew, that's a lot of drugs."

Someone at the next table turns his head. I slide my chair around the table next to her so we can talk more quietly. Anyhow, I like being over here next to her, leaning into the hemisphere of her huge chair. It's as if the two of us are in our own little egg.

"Still, it doesn't explain why you were running down the street."

I let the rest of the story pour out of me. I tell her about how Mandy won all that money in the tournament and how Shushie mentioned her drug problem. I explain how I figured I could make a few bucks to get me back on my feet by selling the stuff to Mandy. I go on to tell her about Mandy's reaction and how I thought she might call the cops.

"You play poker at Shushie Spiegel's place?" Jasmine asks.

His name coming out of her mouth stops me cold. "You know him?" I say.

"Jim does."

"Why, is Jim a big pool player or something? I've never seen him in the card room."

Jasmine shakes her head. "You're such a dunce, Andrew," she says. "Shushie Spiegel is probably the biggest drug dealer in town. Everybody knows that."

"I had no idea."

"Shushie is bad news." Jasmine rolls her tongue barbell between her teeth. It makes a clicking sound that sends chills down my back. "If Mr. Miller had as much as you say on him, he's probably got something going on with Shushie. That's way too much for personal use. It's for sale and distribution. And like I said, Shushie's the biggest dealer in town. I don't know of anyone else who'd handle that much."

"Jesus, I'm so goddamn stupid."

"Do you have the stuff on you?"

I still think she's talking way too loud, but I nod. I take her hand and slide it into my jacket pocket. She grabs the Baggie, and I feel her rolling it around in her palm as if she's working a stress ball.

"Holy shit," she says. "What're you going to do with it?"

"That's the problem. I have no idea."

She pulls her hand out of my pocket and starts to button her coat. "Come on," she says.

"Where're we going?" I toss a few dollars onto the table for my drink.

Jasmine sucks down the rest of her latte. "We have to go see Jim."

F I S H H O O K S

(two jacks)

A **block away** from the police station. That's where Jim lives—a block away from the police station. At least the cops won't have to go far when they come to arrest him for dealing drugs. Jasmine strides at least two steps ahead of me the whole way. Every time I try to catch up, she's out in front again within a few seconds, so I let her lead. Our footsteps make funny squeaking sounds in the snow.

I thrust my hands into the pockets of my coat to fight off the numbness. The Baggie is still there, and the little rocks grind between my fingers.

The snow is still coming down, but the flakes are tiny now, almost like sleet. An icy crust forms on top of the fluffy snow that had fallen earlier.

"Be sure to keep your mouth shut," Jasmine says. "Considering the way Jim and I left things, this isn't going to be easy."

"How did you leave things?"

"Just keep quiet."

"You think Jim might buy it off me cheap?"

"Jim only handles pot."

"Yeah, but he could make a huge profit with this. I only want like a few hundred bucks—just enough to get me on my feet again at the club."

"He doesn't touch crack."

"Yeah but—"

Jasmine whirls around. "Yeah but nothing," she snaps. "We have to figure out a way to deal with this without you getting the shit kicked out of you—or worse."

"What did *I* do wrong? I just found the stuff."

"Look, Mr. Miller knows you have it and probably already told Shushie. Judging from the way that Mandy woman reacted, she's probably already gone to Shushie's and ripped him a new one. How hard do you think it'll be for him to put two and two together? It will look like you're trying to sell Shushie's shit out from under him. So shut up while I try to save your neck."

I shut up.

We walk up an unlit driveway past Jim's Integra. Jasmine presses the doorbell, and the glowing button goes dark. From what I can see, Jim's parents' house is a two-story split-level— white siding atop a brick foundation. Several local circulars in blue plastic bags lie about the porch, uncollected.

"Why are you being so weird about seeing Jim?" I whisper. "He is your boyfriend after all."

Jasmine jerks a thumb at the driveway. "I keyed his car last night when I left the party," she whispers. "Now keep quiet."

"Just deny it," I say. "If he didn't see you, he can't prove anything."

"I scratched 'limpdick' into his new paint job. There's no doubt it was me."

"Anyone could have scratched that there."

"It's what I screamed at him when I stormed out of the party. Now shut up."

I shut up again.

The door opens. Jim is standing there in a baseball cap, sweatpants, and a 50 Cent concert T-shirt that goes almost to his knees. "The fuck you want?" he says to Jasmine. "Come to pay me for a new paint job?"

"It's your own fault."

"It's *my* fault you scratched up my car?"

"What'd you expect after I caught you with that slut?"

"Jesus, we weren't doing nothing."

"Yet," Jasmine says.

The next few seconds feel like hours.

"But forget about that for now," Jasmine says. "Andrew needs your help."

"Who the hell is Andrew?" He looks me over. "What's he, your new boyfriend?" Jim's eyes are just a little too close together and squinty, so I can't tell what part of me he's actually looking over. I wonder what Jasmine sees in this guy anyway. Just being around him makes me want to spew.

"You know who he is," Jasmine says. "The kid I work with."

I hate the word *kid*. *Guy* is a much better word. But now is no time to be picky. If Jim can get me off the hook with Shushie, he can call me Christina Aguilera.

"Why the hell would I want to help his scrawny ass?" Jim says.

Scrawny? I've never been called scrawny before. It's almost funny, though, coming from a guy who's so skinny his Adam's apple pokes out like a vulture's. His hands are so veiny it looks like someone emptied a crate of rubber bands under his skin.

"Come on," Jasmine says.

"You both can go screw yourselves," he says and slams the door in our faces.

Jasmine pounds on the door. "Jimmy, open up. If you help him, you'll probably make enough to get a new paint job and that spoiler you want. Open up."

The door cracks open. "What're you talking about?" Jim says through the gap.

"It has to do with Shushie Spiegel. Just let us in and I'll tell you everything."

Jim swings the door wide and steps back. "You have exactly five minutes."

Jasmine grabs my jacket and tugs me inside. She leads me down the stairs to what must be Jim's room. The smell of pot is strong in here, and it makes me nervous. Don't Jim's parents ever come downstairs?

An unmade twin bed with a rumpled black comforter sits in the far corner opposite a dresser that has a foot-high plaster gargoyle on top. The dark-paneled walls are covered with posters of rappers I've never heard of—real gangsta stuff. A Lava lamp on the nightstand sends purple gloops and globs drifting up and down.

Jasmine sits on Jim's bed. She pats the spot next to her to indicate I should sit down. It's kind of gross thinking about Jim and Jasmine fooling around on this bed, and all of a sudden I don't want to be near it at all. I sit anyway and wonder when Jim last changed his sheets.

"Start talking," he says. He leans against the dresser and begins fidgeting with the brass drawer pulls. "And I'm not kidding about the five-minute thing."

Jasmine tells Jim everything she knows about what's been going on. That is, she tells him everything I've let her in on.

After she finishes, Jim toys with the drawer pulls some more. "What the hell do you want from me?" he asks. "You know I don't touch that stuff. It's bad news. Cops come down on you hard when you deal crack, and it attracts . . . Let's just say it brings around the type of people my mom would definitely have a problem with."

"All I want is for you to straighten this out with Shushie," Jasmine says. "For Andrew."

"Why should I care about him?"

"He's my friend."

Hearing Jasmine call me her friend makes me feel great, like that feeling I had in kindergarten when I was the first kid in class with a pair of those light-up sneakers. I notice I'm sitting up a little taller.

"So you're asking me to help your friend?" Jim says. "You've got a lot of nerve coming around here asking me for anything after last night."

Jasmine's eyes lower toward her laced fingers.

"Or is this to return the favor of you scratching the hell out of my car?" Jim moves forward like he's going to lash out at Jasmine, but she just glares back at him. She doesn't even flinch. I flinch, but she doesn't.

"Listen," I say. I start to get up. "I just—"

"Shut up," Jim says to me. "I don't even know you. Just talking to you about this shit could royally fuck everything up for me."

I sit back down.

Jim turns back to Jasmine. "I can't believe you brought this kid to my house."

"Look," Jasmine says as she gets up. "We'll just get out of here. It was wrong for me to bring him. I just thought you might be able to make this work for you somehow."

"Right," Jim says to her. He crosses his arms and cocks his head to the side, and all of a sudden Jim's lankiness reminds me of the Scarecrow from *The Wizard of Oz*. "I'm sure you're so concerned for my well-being. You're here to piss me off— to get me jealous about this dork over here."

"This was a bad idea," Jasmine says. She starts toward the door. "Come on, Andrew. We'll deal with this some other way."

I follow her, moving in an arc to avoid the radius of Jim's reach.

Then Jasmine puts her hand on the doorknob and mutters the one word even I know she shouldn't: "Limpdick."

Jim growls. Weird, but that's what he does. Jim growls and lunges at Jasmine. I leap forward to get between them, but Jim is too quick. He shoves her hard, and Jasmine's face cracks straight into the edge of the door. The door reverberates with a loud *thwong*, but Jasmine holds on to the doorknob and stays on her feet. She whirls around, blood already streaming from her left nostril. It drips over her lips and makes its way to her chin. A welt is forming over her cheekbone.

"That's the last fucking time!" she screams, blood spattering from her mouth with each word. She shoves Jim hard. He smashes into his dresser, and the gargoyle topples off and shatters on the linoleum floor. Clumps of dried leaves scatter across the floor among the plaster shards. In a berserk rage, Jasmine follows up her shove with a swarm of punches. Jim raises his hands to protect his head, and Jasmine ends up pummeling his shoulder and arms with most of her shots. Her last punch lands on his left temple, and Jim's legs give out. He drops to the floor.

Jasmine kicks him in the side and screams, "Stay down! That's where you belong—with your precious pot. On the ground with your precious fucking pot! That's the last time you'll ever hit me!"

Jim curls up into a ball. "Get the hell out of here!" he cries between his forearms. "Don't ever come here again, you psycho bitch!"

Jasmine kicks him again.

"Stop it," I say. I grab her shoulders and spin her toward the door.

Jasmine drags her sleeve across her face, which is a mess of blood and tears and mucus. "Let's get out of here," she says. She marches up the stairs, and I follow her like the tail of a kite.

By the time I'm halfway to the bottom of the driveway, she's already at the street. The sleet needles my face. All of a sudden, Jasmine spins around and heads back toward the house.

"No," I say. "Let it go." I hold up my hands, but I know she could get by me if she wanted. She knows it, too.

"Fuck him," she wails. With all the eyeliner streaked down her face and the blood and everything, if she didn't look enough like a vampire before, this does the trick. She begins to dig around in her purse, and all of a sudden I'm petrified she's going to pull out a knife or a gun. Visions of my first mug shot flash through my mind.

I grab her shoulders and squeeze. "Calm down," I say. "Jim's had enough. Let's just walk away."

"That's exactly what I'm gonna do," she says between wet sniffs. I hear a jingling from her purse. She pulls out a set of keys. "But I'm not walking." She hits the button on the key fob, and Jim's Acura chirps to life. "Get in."

GERMAN VIRGIN

(two nines)

Jasmine fishtails Jim's canary yellow car out of the driveway and down the icy road. Some rap music filled with angry obscenities is pumping through the speakers. I can feel the bass vibrate my ass in the passenger seat.

Jasmine's cell phone rings. She pulls it from her purse and flips it open. "Fuck off!" she screams and snaps it shut.

"This is a really bad idea," I say.

"Don't be such a wuss," she says. "Jim won't call the cops. He can't. I have too much on him. His room is loaded with pot. Anyhow, we could just tell the police he lent us his car. I have the keys. It's our word against his."

"All I wanted was a few bucks to play poker," I say. "This is way out of control."

Jasmine doesn't say anything. She just keeps driving.

"I'll just go to Shushie and own up to everything," I say. "He'll be thankful I got his stuff back for him. And with any luck, he'll toss me a few bucks to start playing again."

Jasmine sniffles, and I realize she's probably still bleeding—and in a lot of pain. "Jesus," I say, "I'm such an asshole. I didn't even ask if you were okay. Pull over."

Jasmine turns in to the parking lot of the public library and finds a dark space. She leaves the car idling. I fiddle with the stereo knobs to turn down the music, but Jasmine reaches over and hits the Power button before I find the right one.

I turn around and rummage through the junk on the backseat. I find a T-shirt in a duffel bag and hand it to her. She adjusts the rearview mirror and dabs at her face.

"I'm a total mess," she says.

"It's not so bad. Want some snow? It might help with that swelling."

Jasmine shakes her head. "I'll be fine." She works on her face some more, and we let the silence grow between us. The sleet clicking against the glass becomes deafening.

"You brought me to Jim's house to make some kind of point, didn't you?"

"What're you talking about?"

"One thing I've learned playing poker is when someone's feeding me a line of bull," I say. "I could've just as easily gone straight to Shushie. Nothing is going to happen to me. But you dragged me over to Jim's house like I was some kind of trophy."

Jasmine lowers her head. "I'm so screwed up," she says. "I don't know why I did it. I don't know . . ."

"Has Jim hit you before?"

Jasmine doesn't answer.

She presses the side of her fist against the foggy window. It leaves a crescent-shaped imprint. Then with her index finger she makes five small dots above it.

"Look, a baby foot," she says.

It does look like a baby foot. I chuckle and tell myself to show Rooster sometime.

The bruise on Jasmine's face is really coming out now, and her cheek is starting to swell.

I reach for the door handle. "Let me get you some snow."

"Don't worry about it," she says. She grabs my knee to hold me in place.

Her fingers feel like talons, and I freeze.

"Has anybody ever hit you?" she asks.

"Nah," I say. "I remember my dad taking a swing at my mom once, though. I was about five, and they were arguing over the business—how they weren't making enough money. And I remember there was some cancer warning about perchloroethylene—that's the dry-cleaning fluid—"

"No duh," Jasmine says.

"Anyhow, they were fighting over bills, and my father just snapped. He shot out of his chair and screamed for her to shut up. He slapped her right across the face. My mom stared him down until he left. Then she packed our bags and threw me into the car. I was wearing my pajamas. I remember crying about not being able to finish my mac and cheese. We spent a few weeks at my grandmother's house. I don't know, maybe my mom made my father go to therapy or something, but that's the last time he ever raised a hand to any of us. Rooster's never been hit at all."

"Good," Jasmine says. "He's so cute."

Jasmine's hand hasn't left my leg, and suddenly I realize she's looking at me funny. "Andrew," she asks, "have you ever wanted to kiss me?"

My Guy Meets Girl Algorithm springs to mind, and I wonder how I managed to jump so suddenly from one side to the other. I had crossed the thick line down the center!

"What?"

"You know, like at work or something, have you ever wanted to make a move on me?"

Finding myself on the Romantic Response side of my algorithm, I have no idea what to say. I have no idea what to do. I look down at my hand, which is playing with the buttons on the door.

"I've seen how you look at me," she says. "I'm not stupid."

I feel like my brain is short-circuiting, a tangle of buzzing wires. Every moment I hesitate makes it tougher to break the wall of silence. All of a sudden, I'm a million miles away—I'm seeing everything through the wrong end of a telescope.

"Andrew?" she asks. "You there?"

I nod numbly.

"What would you do if I did this?" Jasmine leans in and kisses me. I can taste blood and tears and lip gloss. Her lip ring feels weird against my mouth. But I let it happen. She leans over farther and presses against me. Her tongue explores deeper. It's rougher than I imagined. Her steel barbell clicks against my teeth. I recoil.

"Watch out for that," she whispers. Jasmine's hands make their way to the back of my head and pull my face against hers so tight I feel like she's trying to devour me. She sucks in a huge gulp of air through her nose. Jasmine's fruity smell invades me. I can taste it.

Of all the weird stuff that's happened today, this is the weirdest. I pull myself from her grasp. Her nails scratch like needles across my face. I fling open the door and dart into the night. For the second time today—hell, for the second time in my whole life—I find myself running blindly in a snowstorm with a pocketful of crack.

Sleet bites my cheeks.

Fingers of icy air sneak up my jacket sleeves.

I hear Jasmine's voice calling to me through the swirling wind.

But this time I don't dare turn around.

KING CRAB

(a king and a three)

We got dumped on all night. The plows and snow blowers piled huge mounds of snow around the edges of the parking lot. The pool hall looms above me like that big castle at the beginning of *Scooby Doo*. I usually go in through the back, which leads straight to the basement—to the poker club—but for some reason today the front door feels safer.

After it sat on the shelf in the toolshed overnight, the Baggie of crack in my pocket feels cold. There was no way I was bringing that stuff into the house. With my luck, my mom would've gone on a laundry spree or a cleaning frenzy and found it tucked away someplace. Or worse yet, Rooster would've gotten his snooping little hands on it and I would've been in a big bucket of hot water.

I heave open the door. A blast of warmth assaults me, and I hear the *clack* of billiard balls smacking into one another. I stomp my boots on the rubber mat and head to the door in the back. Ruth, the lady behind the counter, waves me over.

She wrinkles her nose to hoist her glasses into position. "Oh, Andrew, it's you," she says. "Don't usually see your face up here. Go on down."

As I descend the concrete stairwell, my footsteps echo off the walls. It makes the place seem both cavernous and close at the same time, like a prison. I know Shushie is going to be happy to see me, but when I grasp the doorknob I realize my hands are shaking—no, not shaking, rattling.

I open the door, and the odor of the poker room—the mixture of cigarettes, sweat, and fried food—calms me like an embrace. I scan the room for Shushie. As usual, he's crammed behind his desk, chewing on a cigar.

"Andrew, get in here," he calls to me.

I go into his office with the wire-mesh wall. It feels as though I'm being locked in a cage with an angry bear. *It's just Shushie,* I reassure myself, but when I look at him, those words offer no comfort. The choppy scruff covering his pink, pitted skin makes his face look like a rotten tomato that got kicked around the floor of a barbershop.

"Shut the door," he says.

I consider pointing out that one entire wall of his office is a cage and offers no privacy anyway, but I do as he commands.

Shushie pulls the phone from its cradle and hits the intercom button. "Ruth," he says into the receiver. "Tell Alex to get his ass down here." He pauses and rolls the ash stump from his cigar into a coffee cup. "No, not in a few minutes. Now."

I place both hands on the back of a chair and lean forward on it. I want to look at ease, but I'm not comfortable enough to actually sit. "Shushie, I—"

He holds up a hand to silence me and speaks into the phone. "Of course downstairs. Where the hell else?" Shushie hangs up and looks at me. He rocks back in his chair, and it thumps against the wall. Then he exhales through his nose so hard it sounds like the hydraulics on a dump truck. "I understand you have something of mine," he says.

"That's what I came here about." I reach into my coat pocket, but something tells me not to pull the Baggie out just yet. I get the feeling I should have left it hidden someplace safe, like they always do in the movies.

It's just Shushie, I tell myself again.

"I also understand you were trying to unload it all over town."

"Shushie—"

"Shut up," he says. "You're a good kid and you're getting mixed up in something way out of your league." He flips a thumb toward the poker room. "All for what? To play that stupid game?"

"It's not . . ." But I don't finish my thought. I notice all the racket from the poker room—the clicking of chips and the witless banter—has ceased. All I can hear is the low static of the television and a single cough. Everyone is listening.

A knock sounds at the door. "Come on in," Shushie says.

"What do you need?" a voice says. Mr. Miller pokes his head into the office, and Shushie beckons him with a flip of his hand. If it weren't for his caterpillar-like mustache, I wouldn't recognize Mr. Miller. He's wearing a New England Patriots sweatshirt, jeans, and a baseball cap with the bill swung around back. Nothing like the big Wall Street businessman I always see him as.

As soon as Mr. Miller spots me, his expression goes from curious to furious. Then he squeezes out a smile. I can tell he's forcing it because his eyes are still on fire, like he wants to choke me until I stop twitching. "Hey," Mr. Miller says to me. He makes his way to the other chair across from Shushie and sits down. "You know, I've been looking for you. I think I left something in my pocket when I dropped off my clothes yesterday. I stopped back at your dad's place to ask about it, but you'd already left."

"I don't recall," I say. "What did you lose?"

"You little shit," Mr. Miller hisses. He leaps forward and I jump back. I smash into the wire wall with both shoulders. The impact makes a thunderous crash. Someone gasps behind me in the poker room.

"Now, Andrew," Shushie says. "Just give Alex back what's his and all of this will be settled."

This is my only shot at getting the money back in the register, so I really need to make something happen here. But I also know Shushie is right: I *am* way out of my league.

I reach into my pocket, grab the Baggie, and drop it onto the corner of Shushie's desk. Mr. Miller scoops the bag up and scrutinizes it like he's counting each bump on each rock. "It better all be here," he says.

"Shut up," Shushie says to Mr. Miller. "If the kid was going to steal it, he wouldn't be here in the first place. Isn't that right, Andrew?"

I nod.

"Punk," Mr. Miller murmurs. He stuffs the Baggie into his pocket and starts to sit down.

"Hey," Shushie says. It stops Mr. Miller dead, his ass hovering inches above his seat. "Take care of him," Shushie says with a nod to me.

"Take care of him?" Mr. Miller says.

Shushie's chin dips in a single nod.

Take care of me? Visions of concrete shoes and a single shot to the back of the head rush to mind. If I could back up any farther, I would. Instead, I begin to shift from side to side like a cornered rat.

"The kid brought back your stuff," Shushie says. "If he didn't, you'd be into me for four grand. Take care of the kid."

"But he tried to unload it," Mr. Miller says. He sounds whiny, like a ferret getting stepped on with soccer cleats.

"Then he smartened up," Shushie says. "Take care of him."

"How much?" Mr. Miller asks reluctantly.

"A few hundred should do it."

My shoulders relax some, and my body peels away from the wire mesh. I'll probably have pressure imprints for a week.

Mr. Miller yanks a roll of bills from his pocket and strips off two hundreds. He drops them on the desk and turns to leave.

"And don't let me hear about you bothering this kid later on," Shushie says. "Leave him alone. Hell, stay out of his father's place from now on."

"I've been going there for years."

"Find another cleaners. There's one right over here in the next plaza," Shushie says, referring to the new place on the highway. "If I hear you even said another word to him, your arrangement with me is through. Got it?"

"All right." Mr. Miller shoots me a look like I'm the one who left his drugs in his pocket, like I got him into trouble. As soon as the door closes behind him, the din resumes in the poker room.

My lungs deflate, and I sink into one of the chairs. "Thanks, Shush."

"Don't thank me," he says. "This is your one free pass."

Shushie grabs the cash on the desk, takes one of the bills, and tosses the other to me. It flitters onto my lap like a dead leaf on a still autumn day. Shushie stares me down, daring me to say something.

Useless. A hundred is not nearly enough to get me back on my feet. I learned that when I blew all my chips in ten minutes the other day. Three hundred, now that would be easy. Playing conservatively, I could double my money in a few hours with three hundred.

Shit.

I consider protesting. That extra hundred Shushie pocketed could mean all the difference, but I know my mouth needs to stay shut right now.

Shushie picks up his newspaper and rattles it to attention. He grunts. "Jesus, you see this? Some lady's arm got torn off."

He reads me the article. It happened at a Laundromat in Florida. The auto shutoff broke on one of the dryers. The lady's comforter was tumbling around, and she reached in to see if it was dry. Her hand got caught in the wet fabric, and her arm got twisted straight off. She survived because she wrapped a belt around her arm and held it with her teeth.

Nasty.

On any other day, the article might warrant a full conversation. Today, I'm all about business. I toss the bill back onto Shushie's desk. "How about some chips?" I say.

Shushie's head pokes up from behind his paper, but he doesn't even glance at the money. He looks straight into my eyes. "No can do, Andrew. You're cut off."

"Cut off?"

"You heard me."

"Why?"

"It's like I told you last time. It was stupid of me to let you play here in the first place. Eventually the heat will come down on me. And after all this drug shit . . ."

"Shush, I didn't know—"

"There's no arguing this. My mind is made up. You're out of here."

"Just this one last time," I say. "I have to make up some lost ground."

Shushie lifts his shoulders and lets them drop, the newspaper still clutched in his pudgy hands. "And that's my problem because . . . ?"

There's no answer to a question like that. Absolutely no answer. I swipe up my hundred and stuff it into my pocket.

"Look, kid," Shushie says. "You've got a lot of potential. Go to college. Get an education. Don't end up like all the other derelicts who waste their lives sitting at the felt. Do something useful with your life."

A lecture. Shushie is giving me a goddamn lecture. I would expect this from my father. I would expect this from my guidance counselor. But getting a lecture from a guy rotting away in the basement of a pool hall is too much.

I yank the zipper of my coat all the way up and head out of the office. The door slams behind me harder than I intended, and it quiets the poker room again. Heads turn, but in an instant all the gazes drift back down to the cards.

All but one.

Mandy continues to stare at me across the room. It's one of those stares that feels like it's going through you, like it can see something you don't want it to see—something too personal to share with anyone else. She's sitting at the far corner table. Her eyes are so sunken she looks like a phantom. She mouths the word *Sorry*, then looks back down at her hand like all the other cattle.

I would give anything to be one of them again.

I want to scream, but I don't. I head out into the gloom of Sunday morning and realize I have absolutely nowhere to go but home.

BASKIN-ROBBINS

(a three and an ace)

Andrew!" Rooster squeals. He sprints from the kitchen right into me. His arms wrap around my waist, and he tries to heave me into the air like a pro wrestler. I topple over onto the living room couch. Rooster scrambles behind me and snakes his arm around my neck in a perfect headlock. I taught him that.

I tap the sofa cushion three times. "I give up," I wail and roll him off my shoulders.

The television is roaring in the family room, but not loud enough to drown out my father's voice. "Good, you're home," he calls. "The driveway needs shoveling."

"In a little bit."

"The sooner you do it, the lighter it is. Try to get to it before it turns to lead."

I drop the conversation by not answering. I wait a few seconds to make sure the pregame coverage draws his attention back.

"What're you doing?" I ask Rooster.

"You're all wet."

"Yeah, I know. What're you doing?"

"And you smell."

"You smell worse," I say and lightly knuckle him in the shoulder.

"You smell like cigarettes again, just like the other night when Dad got mad." Rooster sits up like his spine is a Popsicle stick and looks at his knees.

"What?"

He gets a real worried look and squints at me through his glasses. "We learned at school that cigarettes make you die."

"I'm not going to die," I say. "I don't even smoke. What're you up to?"

"I was watching *Power Rangers*, but Dad wants to watch football. Mom said we could bake cookies. She's letting me push down the cookie cutters and decorate a bunch of cookies with frosting and sprinkles and M&M's and Red Hots. I'm going to make a whole train—a caboose and everything. We bought the cookie cutters at the store. Mom let me pick them out."

"Cool."

"Want to make some, too? Mom'll give you some dough."

"Nah, I have homework to do."

"I'll bring you some when they're all decorated."

"Thanks, Roo." I make my way up the stairs, praying with every step I won't receive the official summons from my father. I just want to go crash for a few hours without getting the third degree about leaving the house so early this morning. I got up before anyone, even Rooster, and walked around in the snow for a while before I went to Shushie's. My parents are both pretty occupied, but I still get that electric feeling across my shoulders like one of them is going to call my name. I try to walk lightly.

"And Dad said we're going to condition Yoko's seats later

on," Rooster calls after me. "We're heating up the garage now."

"I'll pass."

My father has called his antique muscle car Yoko since my grandfather gave it to him as a high school graduation gift. He even had the name painted in fancy white letters right over the door handle. I think nowadays if someone called their car Yoko they'd get their ass kicked, or at least their car would get egged all the time. Not that anyone would ever have the chance to egg Yoko; my father only takes her out two or three times a year when the temperature and humidity are just right.

Fat chance my parents will give me a car when I graduate. I'll be lucky to get a day off from the cleaners to go up to Lake George. Then it occurs to me: *or to the casino.* Since the Indian casinos don't serve alcohol, you only have to be eighteen to play. I'll be able to play poker legally in less than two years.

I toss my coat on my desk chair and plop onto my unmade bed. Now that I'm lying still, I can smell the smoke on my clothes, too. I pull off my shirt and stuff it into the hamper.

All I want to do is pass out. Physically, I'm exhausted, but my head is ready to explode. My brain feels like it needs more space to do all the thinking that's going on up there.

How am I going to act toward Jasmine at work on Monday? Did I screw everything up by running off? What is she thinking right now?

And the money that has to get back into the register . . .

And I can't go back to Shushie's . . .

And Scott . . .

Shit.

Shit, shit, shit!

I feel like a rhinoceros is sitting on me.

A knock sounds on the door. It's a Mom Knock, light and tentative, telling me she'll go away if I ignore it.

But I don't.

"Uh-huh," I say as I pull on a shirt.

The door opens no more than an inch or two.

"Mind if I come in?" she asks.

"Sure."

My mom opens the door just wide enough for her to slip into the room. She closes the door behind her as silently as James Bond sneaking around the bad guy's fortress to find the stolen microfilm. Then she waggles a slip of white paper in the air. "Scott called." She places the note next to my phone.

"Thanks."

"He sounded . . . strange." She looks down at the floor. "Like something was on his mind. Is everything okay with him?"

"Fine, I guess."

Mom moves across the room. Actually, she glides. Now that I think about it, I never hear her feet on the carpet—a skill she probably gained from too many years around my father. I do the same thing.

God, my conversation with Jasmine really churned up a lot of old stuff. All I want to do right now is ask my mom about what really happened with my father when she took me to my grandmother's house all those years ago.

But of course I don't.

Mom sits on the edge of my bed and rests her hand on my back. Her hand kind of flutters a little before it finds its place, and it makes me feel weird. She never touches. I guess she's trying, so I don't move away. But I still get this creepy-crawly feeling, and I think she can tell because her hand leaves my shoulder and joins the other one in her lap.

"Have you ever heard of Sudoku?" she asks.

"That grid thing with the numbers? I've seen it but never looked too closely."

She nods. "I thought you might like it. It's right up your alley."

She starts wringing her hands like she's trying to strangle the life out of her own fingers. The small diamond on her engagement ring bobs around like a picket sign. "So, what's going on?" she asks.

Everything gets heavy. The air itself feels heavy. My vision gets fuzzy around the edges, and I start to hear a whooshing noise, like static, in my head. "Going on with what?" I ask, but I don't feel myself say it. It's more like I'm watching myself from somewhere else.

My mom breathes out through her nose in that frustrated sort of way. Her breath drifts across me, and the little hairs on my forearm stand to attention.

"Don't make this difficult, Andrew. I know something's bothering you. You haven't been yourself. Is it something with Scott?"

"No," I say. "I'm fine. Scott's fine."

I can tell she doesn't believe me.

"Serious," I say. "I've just been a little tired."

"Of course you're tired," she says. "You don't get home until late most nights. This morning you were out of here just after dawn. The way you've been doing in school, I can't imagine you've been spending all that time studying."

"Mom, it's just that stupid English class. Mr. David hates me."

"Is it that card game? Are you playing that card game with Scott all the time?"

I know she's talking about Four Horsemen, but it strikes me as funny how close to being right she is. Like everything else my mom thinks she knows about me, she's close but still way off. And realizing that makes me feel farther away from her than ever.

"No, it's not that card game," I say. I drop an annoyed tone into my voice. That usually gets her to back off. "We barely play Four Horsemen anymore."

She rises and moves over to my desk. This time I can hear her footsteps. "Andrew, how can I help if you won't tell me what's going on?" Her voice cracks a little like she really means it.

"Help with what?"

"I don't know. You go to school, then to God knows where, and then come home and go to sleep."

"You forgot working at the hellhole, too."

"Well, that, too." She leans against my desk chair and runs her hands over my jacket—the jacket that until about an hour ago had a bag of crack in the pocket. My mother doesn't know anything about me anymore.

"You know," she says. "I remember when you were Rooster's age—God, you must've been younger than Rooster. He's getting so big. Anyhow, you were out back behind the toolshed. I was picking up leaves, and I heard a loud *pop* back where you were. The first thing that came to my mind was *gun*. I dropped my rake and came running. There was a fire burning in the dried leaves right next to that rusty, old gas can for the lawn mower. After I saw you were fine, I screamed at you. God, did I scream. You scared me half to death. I think I scared *you* half to death with all my screaming."

I start smiling. "What was I doing out there?"

"You had taken a roll of cap gun caps, dunked them in the gas, and dropped a brick on them. The thing went off like a gunshot and lit the leaves on fire."

"Good one," I say.

"Yeah, great," she says. "That leaky gas can was right next to the fire. You could've been killed. Anyway, you ran to the couch—that ugly orange striped couch we had. You started crying and carrying on about how I didn't love you anymore." A smile stretches across tight lips, and her face gets kind of blotchy like she's holding back a cry and it's all building up in her face.

My vision gets even fuzzier than before, and I start staring at the pattern on my comforter. If I squint my eyes right, the black houndstooth looks like rows of clubs and spades.

"When people have babies," my mother continues, "you always hear them say how they love that baby more than they love themselves. I told myself that, too. I thought it in my head over and over. But I never really understood it until I threw myself at that can of gasoline. My own safety didn't even cross my mind."

The clubs and spades fade, and all I can see is the criss-cross pattern again.

I look at her leaning against my desk chair. Her hands are clenched to the edge of my desk so hard I can see her knucklebones straining against the inside of her skin. The corner of the hundred-dollar bill is sticking out of my jacket pocket right next to her arm.

"I just want you to know that you can come to me about anything, no matter how bad you think it is," she says.

I nod.

She puts a hand on my shoulder, and it doesn't feel nearly as bad as the last time.

"I have to get back downstairs before Rooster wrecks the kitchen," she says. She moves to the door.

"Hey, Mom?" I say.

She looks at me expectantly. "Yes?"

"Make me an angel."

"What?"

"Make me an angel," I say. "One of your famous cookie angels with a Red Hots halo and frosted wings."

"You got it," she says. This time her smile reminds me of a clothesline: thin, taut, and weighed down with everyone else's wet laundry.

I feel as though I've helped her in some weird way. As if her baking me a cookie is going to make it all better. But after she leaves, I realize that not even a cookie angel with a Red Hots halo and frosted wings could help me at this point. There's only one thing that can help me, and it's a different kind of dough altogether.

Then the idea hits me like a flyswatter. I know what I need to do.

C O W B O Y S

(two kings)

The first thing that catches my eye is the smear of dried pizza
sauce down the pale green of the living room wall. It
seems like years ago that I threw that slice at Scott. The sauce
is dark, like dried blood, but there's no mistaking it. The sight
brings with it a heaviness—a sense of dread. I squash that
feeling and focus on what I'm here to do. I suck in a deep
breath, a breath deeper than the fear, and wipe my feet on the
mat.

Why does Scott insist on leaving his front door unlocked,
anyway? I've asked him about it, and he says his family has
never locked the door. It must be a midwestern thing. They
must trust each other more out there. I have no idea if
Cincinnati is in the Midwest. Either way, Scott should lock
the stupid door.

Something in me cries out to get a sponge and scrub the
wall. I squash that feeling, too.

I run my fingers through my hair to shake the sleety mist
from it and move from the living room to the hallway. Scott
calls it a hallway, but it's more like a room that all the other
rooms branch off of—like a hub.

I don't know why I'm tiptoeing. It's not like anyone's
home. Scott goes to the comic book shop every Sunday to

play in the Four Horsemen tournament. He never misses it. And when Mr. Oberlin isn't on one of his business trips, he mostly stays at his girlfriend's place. Anyhow, the car is not in the driveway. There's no one here. I call "hello" anyway. If someone happens to be home, I can just say I was looking for Scott.

The house feels like it's been abandoned. It smells like Scott's house, though. There's no mistaking that. It's not a bad odor, it just smells like guys live here—like no one ever thought about opening a window or spraying some air freshener around.

I tiptoe into Mr. Oberlin's bedroom. I figure the money drawer must be the uppermost one in the tall dresser. I open it up and start rummaging around. With the gloom outside and the shades pulled all the way down, I can't see anything except the dark silhouettes of rolled-up socks. I wonder if I could get away with turning on the light. I wonder if any of the neighbors would notice. I wonder about that nosy lady next door who's always poking her head out and giving me nasty looks. I make a mental map of the neighborhood and think about which way Mr. Oberlin's bedroom faces. The nosy lady lives on the opposite side; she can't even see these windows.

I switch on the nightstand lamp and blink a few times until my eyes adjust to the intensity of the bare bulb. Then I return to the dresser and peer into the drawer. Around forty pairs of rolled-up dress socks, all black and navy blue, sit in neat rows, like a tray of freshly baked buns. A single pair of white athletic socks is tucked on the right side. A burgundy jewelry box rests all the way in the back, and a thick, ceramic mug loaded with loose change is wedged in the front corner.

I open the jewelry box and catch the glint of two watches and a gold wedding band. I lift out the velour-covered cardboard thing from the box to look underneath. Empty. I pull out the little jewelry box drawer. Nothing aside from a few tie tacks and a pair of cuff links. No one wears cuff links anymore.

I shut the box. The sound echoes off the walls and startles me. A nervous chuckle escapes my lips, and I remind myself there's nothing to be worried about. I grope around the edges of the drawer. Bare wood. I dig with my hands under the socks. Still nothing.

I think back to when Scott came in here the other night to get money for the pizza guy. I'm certain he walked to the tall dresser. Maybe it was one of the other drawers. I pull them out one by one and send my hands searching for the feel of money, for the feel of anything that's not old guy clothes.

Just to make sure, I check the two drawers in the nightstand. The top one holds a Bible, a notepad, and a pen. The lower one is loaded with pornography. A Bible and porn. I let out another chuckle and take a moment to glance at the covers of the magazines. Crinkled and ragged around the edges, the *Playboy* issue with Madonna sits right on top. It's an old one—over twenty years. I didn't know Madonna was that old—she's got to be like my mom's age. The thought of Mr. Oberlin looking at these magazines makes me want to hurl, and I shut the drawer.

I sit on the edge of the queen-size bed and think about Mr. Oberlin for a second. *Where would he hide money?* World history and quantum physics books. La-Z-Boys. He's kind of a boring guy. Not totally boring, but exactly like you'd expect an electrical engineer to be. Dry and straightforward. *Straightforward.*

I go back to the top drawer of the tall dresser. Something wasn't quite right in here the first time. White socks. One pair of white socks. My hand finds the white athletic socks and squeezes them. I feel a crunchy sort of feeling inside. I unroll the socks, and a wad of money wrapped with a rubber band tumbles out. It's no small amount, either. It's like those rolls you see gangsters pull out of their pockets in Mafia movies.

I count it. It's mostly fives and tens, all crisp, new, and facing the same direction. Three hundred and fifty dollars. Along with the hundred I already have, it's almost enough to balance the register. Almost. But if there's still money missing on Monday, even if it's only $150, Dad is going to have a freak attack. If only I could play at Shushie's. I could turn $450 into a grand in a few hours, maybe less.

Then it occurs to me. If I take all of it, Scott's likely to notice right away. And his dad's gonna notice, too. And all hell is gonna break loose. Scott knows I've been gambling, and he might put two and two together. If I take some of it, a hundred or so, maybe no one will notice. But then I'm still screwed. The register is going to be way short.

I hear a sound—no, I feel a force—behind me. It's like a *thump, thump, thump.* The force approaches me like a wave. Before I have a chance to turn, someone barrels into me. My head snaps back whiplash style, and the roll of cash pops from my hand. I fall to the carpet. Scott is on top of me in an instant, punching, pounding, and slapping, amid a flurry of five- and ten-dollar bills.

"You asshole!" he screams over and over. At first he's hitting me way faster than he's screaming the words, but after a while he develops a sort of cadence where each *asshole* is accompanied by a punch.

I focus on the rhythm and cover my face.

I let Scott keep on hitting me because I know he's right—I *am* an asshole. I let him get it all out. I'm wearing my heavy jacket anyway, and it absorbs most of the force.

And he hits like a girl. Actually, Jasmine hits harder.

Finally, when his arms give out, he drops to the carpet and rolls onto his back, panting.

"I'm sorry, Scott," I say, and it's now that I realize I'm crying. My words come out between a mixture of sobbing and wheezing and sucking in air. "I'm screwed. I don't know what to do. I'm so screwed!"

Scott doesn't say anything. Still panting, he gets up and sits on the edge of the bed. The lamp on the nightstand illuminates only half his face, like something out of an artsy French film or a fancy perfume commercial.

"My father is going to kill me," I manage to say. I start to pick up the money, putting it back into a neat and ordered stack, like it was before Scott whaled into me.

"What do you care what your father's going to say?" Scott finally asks. His breathing has settled down a little. "Why do you care at all?"

My eyes don't leave the money. I keep organizing it. And I try to take a few deep breaths to stop my chest from sucking in those uncontrollable sobs.

"You shit on me," Scott says. "That's what you did. You shit on my whole family."

"Scott, I don't know what to do." The sobs really come

now, and I cover my face with my hands. Scott is the last person I want to see me cry. I'm always so in control around him. I'm the strong one, not him.

"You're always bitching about working at the cleaners," Scott says. "Everyone knows that's not what you want to do with your life. Let your father find the money missing. Let him go ballistic. He'll fire you. So what? You'll get grounded. So what?"

"Maybe that's what you'd do," I say, still not looking up at him. My breathing is jittery, and it comes in through my words. "Your father leaves money for you rolled up in his socks, like they're goddamn Easter eggs."

"You make such a big deal out of everything—like somehow your life is so much more important. Like everyone else has it so easy." Scott is really worked up now. He's leaning forward, and little bits of spittle are flying from his mouth onto my jacket. I don't dare wipe them off, though.

"My life sucks, Andrew. I come home to this." He sweeps his hands around, gesturing to the house. "I eat microwave dinners five nights a week and hope to find someone to go out with the other two. I fall asleep in front of the television every night and oversleep for school almost every day. I'd trade with you in a second. I wish I had someone on my ass all the time. I feel like an abandoned dog more than a son."

I had never thought about it that way. I never knew Scott was so unhappy. He never complains about anything. He just chugs along like his life is going great. Half the time I expect him to break into song, like a guy in *Oklahoma!* or something.

I wrap the rubber band around the money and stick it back into the socks just like I found it.

"If that money's so important to you," Scott says, "if you're in that much of a bind that you'd steal from your best friend, then keep it. I'll take the heat. I don't care."

A semblance of a smile grows from within me. Best friend. Scott is my best friend. Jesus, I don't think I've treated him like one in months. He comes by the cleaners almost every day, and I blow him off to play poker. He calls every night and IMs me obsessively. Yet up until now, I've never seen him as more than a nuisance.

I drop the socks with the money back into the drawer. "No," I say. "Keep the money."

"No, really. If you need it, take it."

"Thanks. I appreciate it. I really do . . . but—"

"But what?"

"It's not enough."

"Jesus," he says. "How much do you need?"

"Six hundred."

Scott looks at me like my face just turned purple paisley. "There's a few hundred in the sock," he says. "Play poker with it. You can probably turn it into six hundred before you know it. If it's what you think you have to do, take it."

"I'm locked out at Shushie's. I can't play there anymore."

"What happened?"

I tell him. I take off my jacket, sit on the floor, and tell him. I don't leave out a single thing. Of course, Scott wants me to elaborate on every detail when it comes to Jasmine and me in the Integra, but the rest of the story keeps him on the edge of the bed, too.

And when I'm done, a single word escapes his lips.

"Shit."

I look down. My hands are in my lap trying to strangle each other, just like my mom's were earlier.

"Shit what?" I say.

"Shit, I can't believe you did all that wild stuff without bringing me along."

"You would've wanted to be in the backseat when Jasmine was mauling me?"

"Hell yeah!" Scott says. He tosses off his jacket and starts pacing.

I lean back against the wall and stretch out my legs. They go halfway across the room, and Scott has to step over them with every lap.

"I've tried to watch Texas Hold 'Em on television a bunch of times, but I could never get into it," he says.

"Yeah, it takes some time to appreciate. It's not the rules that make it interesting. It's the betting."

"Teach me."

"Teach you? What good's that going to do?"

"If you can't play at Shushie's, then I will. I'm good at Four Horsemen. How much harder can it be?"

"If you're so good at Four Horsemen, then why are you home so early?"

"Okay, I sucked today, but usually I'm good at it."

"Look, Scott, it takes a long time—months, even years—to be a profitable poker player. If you go in there, if you even get past the front door, which I doubt you would, you'd lose your whole bankroll in fifteen minutes. They'd eat you up like sharks in a chum slick."

"Then we'll just have to find another place for you to play," Scott says, opening the top drawer of the tall dresser. He pulls out the white socks and stuffs the whole wad in his pocket. "I'm all packed—money and socks."

"Where're we going?" I ask.

"How about Crystal Waters, that Indian casino?"

"You have to be eighteen to get in."

"Kids get in there all the time. A few weeks ago, Sam Carchman lost five hundred dollars in like fifteen minutes playing blackjack. Tell your mom you're staying here tonight."

"I don't know," I say. "How're we going to get there?"

"Call Jasmine," Scott says like he's been planning this for weeks. "See if she's still got Jim's wheels. I've got the cash; she's got the ride. It's karma, dude!" As Scott gets more excited, he starts pacing faster. "We'll drive out there." He looks at his watch. "We can be there by six. You'll play cards all night while Jasmine and I drop a few bucks into the slots. We'll be home in time for school tomorrow morning."

Call Jasmine. The thought of calling Jasmine makes my lungs tighten up and squeeze all the air from my chest. I do know her cell number. She wrote it on a piece of masking tape in thick Magic Marker and stuck it to her phone so she wouldn't forget. I see it so often it's burned into my memory.

"What if they card us?" I say.

Scott shrugs. "We come home. Who cares? It's worth a shot." He tosses the cordless phone into my lap. "Call her."

I dial Jasmine's number before I give myself a chance to think of a reason not to.

D U C K S

(two twos)

Every ring of the phone makes me more edgy. I remind myself of the phone calls I make at the cleaners to nag people to pick up their stuff. The first few times I did those calls, I was terrified. I had no idea what to say. Now I make them without a second thought. Calling girls will never be that easy for me, but thinking about it that way helps a little. At least I can breathe again.

Someone picks up.

"I'll bring back your stupid car when I'm good and ready!" she says.

It's Jasmine—loud and clear.

Before I have a chance to say anything, she hangs up.

I hit the Power button and toss the phone on the bed.

"What happened?" Scott asks.

"She thought it was Jim."

"Call her again," Scott says and motions to the receiver. I notice a familiar glint in his eyes—the I-don't-care-what-anyone-thinks-because-I-have-a-good-idea-and-I'm-gonna-see-it-through-to-the-end look of the Scott I know.

Reluctantly, I pick up the phone and hit Redial.

Jasmine picks up, and before she has a chance to say anything, I say, "Jasmine, it's me. It's Andrew."

There's a long pause. She's either confused or angry. I slide my finger to the Power button so I can hang up if she starts freaking out on me.

"Andrew?" Her voice is calm and turns up at the end, like she's talking to a puppy.

"Where are you?" I say.

"At home. My parents are out Christmas shopping. I'm keeping Jim's car awhile. He's lucky I'm not rolling it into the Hudson River." There's a long pause. Then she continues. "Andrew, I'm so sorry about last night. I don't know . . . I was just so freaked out by—"

"It's okay," I say. "It's me who freaked out."

"Yeah but—"

"Don't worry about it," I say. Then I pause to gather some confidence. The dots on the ceiling tiles start to dance. I count how many are in each row and column—fourteen by fourteen. I multiply. A hundred and ninety-six dots per tile. "Scott and I have an idea, but—"

"You fixed things with Scott?"

"Yeah, everything's cool with us." I multiply out the tiles on the ceiling—ten by twelve—a hundred and twenty.

"Good, I was worried about you guys."

Scott comes over and tries to pry the phone from my hand. "Let me ask her," he hisses. "The suspense is killing me."

I push him away and whisper for him to shut up.

"Ask me what?" she says. I can hear the smile in her voice.

I try to multiply the number of ceiling tiles by the number of dots on each tile—a hundred and ninety-six times a hundred and twenty. The math is too hard for me to do in my head, but I manage to come up with the last two numbers—a two and a zero.

"Hello?" Jasmine asks.

"Scott and I have an idea," I say, "but it'll only work if you're in."

"What's your idea?"

As I tell her, it sounds like the stupidest thing I've ever thought of doing. Stupider than dunking caps in gasoline and dropping a brick on them. Stupider than jumping off the roof with a pillowcase parachute. Stupider than peeing down the stairs to see what step I could reach. Stupider than using the CB in the school multimedia room to curse out truckers. Stupider than trying to sell a Baggie of stolen drugs.

We would be three underage high school students driving in a stolen car to a casino in order to play poker with sort of stolen money. Mega-stupid.

But this is one of those ideas that grows. It's the kind of idea that starts off as a whim but quickly turns into a mission. Before you know it, the mission becomes an obsession—like it has to be done at the cost of our lives. The more I think about it, the more I'm sure we have to get to Crystal Waters Casino. I'd be lying if I said it doesn't have anything to do with the money. I'd be lying if I said it doesn't have anything to do with playing poker. But there's something else. Something stronger than those things is pulling me.

When I finish telling Jasmine our idea, silence fills the other end of the line.

"Hello?" I say.

"Yeah, I'm here."

"So, are you in?"

"Jesus, Andrew, I would never have guessed you'd steal from your dad's place."

"Yeah," I say. "It's been a weird few weeks."

"I'll say." I hear a tapping on the line, like she's drumming her fingers on the receiver. "Are you guys serious about this?"

"Very."

She exhales. It's one of those exhales that means she's thinking things over. While she thinks, I go back to multiplying out the number of dots in the ceiling tiles. The third digit from the right is a five. Scott sits on his father's bed, probably to give his knees free rein to pump up and down.

"I'll pick you guys up at the cleaners," Jasmine says. "How's fifteen minutes?"

As we make our way to the cleaners, all I can think about is how cold it is. Every tiny gap in my clothing lets in an ice dagger that slices across my skin. I hunch up my shoulders and tuck my head partway into the neck of my coat, turtle style. Scott rushes alongside me, but hardly a word passes between us. It's as though opening our mouths would waste too much body heat. The cleaners materializes from the swirling darkness, and once I see it, I push myself faster.

I don't see the yellow Integra in the parking lot. Jasmine's not here yet.

"Let's go inside," I say. I key into the building and deactivate the alarm. It chirps into submission. Scott reaches for the lights, but I grab his wrist.

"Leave them off. The cops watch this place close. My dad cleans their uniforms at a discount and donates money to the

Police Athletic League so they can go to some competition in Arizona every year."

Scott nods and lowers his hand.

The heat in the cleaners is on an electronic timer so it's only about sixty, but it sure beats the negatives outside.

"Think Jasmine'll actually show up?" Scott says. He boosts himself onto the counter.

"Yup."

Scott's heels bump and thump against the cabinets. I wonder if his legs ever stop.

"I mean, why wouldn't she come?" I add.

"You're right. It's only been ten minutes. When a girl says fifteen, it means more like thirty—maybe longer."

My eyes start to follow the course of the steam pipes. A single, thick cylinder emerges from the floor and branches in all sorts of directions until it reaches each machine. I've traced the pipes with my eyes a thousand times. I think I could rebuild the whole thing if someone took it apart and gave me a wrench and a half hour.

A long beam of light stretches obliquely across the store, and I hear heavy tires crunch through the snow. I press my face to the window and see a halo of yellow around two lights. It's Jim's car. The engine shuts off, and a single figure rushes toward the building.

I open the door and Jasmine comes in. Her face looks better than it did yesterday. I can still see swelling, though. She probably covered most of the bruising with makeup.

"Jeez, it's cold out there." Jasmine tears off her jacket and tosses it and her purse next to Scott on the counter. She steps on the pedal, and the racks come to life. "Now let's find some clothes to wear."

Scott and I glance at each other. "Huh?" I say.

"You don't think you can just waltz into a casino wearing sweats, do you? If we look like we're on our way to a high school basketball game, they're going to card us. Scott, you're about Mr. Amato's size. He dresses pretty cool."

She rolls the rack around and stops in the A section. Pulling off a large bundle of clothing, she hoists it onto the rolling rack and starts digging through the pieces. She selects a pair of khakis, a cobalt blue dress shirt, and a charcoal three-button wool sportcoat.

"Put these on," she tells him.

Scott looks at me and shrugs.

I shrug back.

He takes the clothes and disappears into the back of the store. Jasmine steps on the pedal again.

"Hey," Scott calls over the din of the squeaking racks. "What's the difference between pants, slacks, and trousers?"

Jasmine and I answer at the same time. "Nothing!"

"Really?" he says. "Slacks sound like they have a sharp crease, and trousers sound all wrinkly to me."

"Trousers are what crotchety old guys call their pants," I say. "Slacks are what the old guys' wives call their husbands' trousers. Pants are what everybody else calls them. Everyone who's normal."

"Gotcha," Scott says.

Jasmine lifts her foot off the pedal. She hangs a few things on the bar next to the front counter. "You're about Mr. Perry's size," she says. "You'll look good in these."

"Thanks."

"I have to find myself a dress," Jasmine says. "What do you think, red or black?"

I've never seen Jasmine in anything but black. In fact, it's what she's wearing right now—black turtleneck, black skirt, and black leggings.

"Red," I say.

A wry smile curls up on her face. "I had a feeling you'd say that." She turns to the rack. "Mrs. Bonneau brought in a great red dress last week. Let me look."

The racks start spinning again, and I rush to the back with my clothes.

When I get to my father's desk, Scott is busy stuffing his shirttails into his pants. Jasmine was right; the outfit does look good on him. Aside from eighth-grade graduation, I've never seen Scott in a jacket. It makes him look—I don't know—it makes him look sort of snazzy.

"You look like an idiot," I say.

"Oh, shut up." Scott sits on my father's chair and puts his feet up on the desk. Old basketball pool sheets flutter to the ground. "Get to work or you're fired!" he says in his surliest voice, which isn't surly at all.

"Bite me."

I strip the plastic off the clothes Jasmine picked out for me. She chose black pants, a powder yellow shirt with charcoal pinstripes in a tight grid pattern, and a hip-length black leather jacket. If I shrug right, the shirt and jacket pull taut across my shoulders, and the pants are a bit long. Otherwise, everything fits great. I survey my reflection in the bathroom mirror and I barely recognize myself.

"Pretty cool," Scott says. "You look like a skinny Tony So-prano."

"I feel like him."

"You sure you want to do this?"

I think about the money I took from the register. It seems so trivial now. Six hundred dollars. I could own up to what I did and pay my father back in a few weeks. Now that I'm banned from Shushie's, I've got no place to spend my pay-check. I think about my father—how he's going to ricochet off the walls when he balances the books. After everything that's happened in the past few days, even his fury seems in-significant. All that matters to me now is this trip to the casino.

"Absolutely positive," I say. "I usually don't like your ideas, but this one seems inspired."

"Thanks." Scott pokes me in the shoulder with a playful punch. "I hope I didn't hurt you too bad before. You know, back at my house."

"All my teeth are still there, right? I think I'll pull through."

I weave my way to the front of the store. Jasmine's back is to me, and she's pulling her dress up over her hips. I can see the strap of her red bra span her back, and I avert my eyes.

"Would you zip this up?" she says, backing up to me.

My hands tremble as I zip her up. Jasmine spins around like a runway model. The dress is knee length. It's low cut with narrow, beaded shoulder straps. The silk flows around her like the dress was made for her—like she and the dress are more than the sum of their parts. And the black choker with a single silver heart she produces from her purse makes the perfect accessory.

"You—" I say. "You look different."

"Different good or different bad?" She smoothes the material along her belly to her thighs and glances down the length of her body.

"Definitely different good."

"Thanks. My panty hose and heels are in my bag. These combat boots won't do at the casino. Hey, you don't look too bad yourself."

Scott shoulders through the clothes hanging near the pressing machine. "You guys going to the prom or something?"

My face gets hot.

A car door slams.

All three of our heads swivel toward the front, and we duck behind the counter. Scuffling sounds come from outside, and a pair of headlights crawls across the front of the store. It looks like a black Corolla. The headlights of the Integra flicker to life and the engine starts. Jim's car pops into gear and begins to roll backward.

"That son of a bitch!" Jasmine says.

She leaps forward, but I grab her. She struggles with me, but I press her against the counter and make her stay put.

"You going to throw snowballs at his taillights?" I say. "Let him go. It's not worth it."

"Yeah," Scott adds. "Jim's a jackass anyway."

Jasmine struggles some more, then twists from my grip. Fortunately, she pulls herself together and doesn't go tearing out into the snow. "You don't even know him," she says to Scott.

"Sure I do. Freshman year, he put an egg in the front of my pants. He yelled 'Cock-a-doodle-doo,' you know, stressing the *cock* part, and smashed the egg with his hand."

Jasmine's eyes lock on to mine as we both try to suppress smiles.

"Go ahead," Scott says. "Laugh it up."

He boosts himself onto one of the laundry baskets piled high with clothes. His heels don't bounce. In fact, his legs are completely still. "So, now what?" Scott asks.

"Yeah," Jasmine says. "We're all dressed up and no place to go."

"We're still going," I say. "We have to get to Crystal Waters Casino one way or another."

"We don't have any wheels," Jasmine says.

She and Scott look at me with curious expressions—like they see something in my face that I don't yet realize is there. Then I notice the name bouncing around inside my head. Over and over, the same name.

"Yes we do," I say. "We just have to do a little shoveling first."

"Shoveling?" Scott says. "I don't even shovel at my own house. What're we going to do?"

And the word—the name—that was rattling around comes out, and once it does I know what Scott said about karma is absolutely right. Everything is falling into place.

"Yoko," I say. "We're going to take Yoko."

MAXWELL SMART

(an eight and a six)

My father was right: shoveling is much easier if you do it right away. Day-old snow feels like lead. Each scoop sticks to the shovel and wrenches my back with every heave-ho. Yoko's garage is back behind the house, so we have a lot of work to do. With the three of us, though, we're getting through the job quickly.

"Good thing I have my boots," Jasmine says. "This would've been ten times harder—and colder—in heels."

Scott plunges his shovel into the snow. "You know, I saw on the news that if you spray your shovel with cooking oil, the snow slides off easier."

"Shut up and keep working," I say as I heave another load into the bushes.

"I saw it on television," he says. "It has to be right."

I estimate the amount of time it will take to go inside, pull off my boots, find the cooking spray, put my boots back on, and spray our shovels. I compare it with how much time we might save if what Scott saw on television works. Then I factor in the possibility of running into my father. It's not worth it. I'm sure we can roll the car down the driveway in neutral without my father hearing, but running into him in the house might get me to wuss out.

Jasmine plants her shovel in the snow. "You gonna fetch the cooking oil or what?" I can see her breath in the yellow glow of our porch light. I want to capture that air in a jar and keep it on my shelf.

"You serious?" I ask her. "You really want me to go for cooking spray?"

"If it'll save us time, I'm serious as hell."

I drop my shovel and head up the walk toward the house. "No one take my shovel. I like that one."

"Yeah, whatever." Scott is already swapping his with mine.

My mother keeps the house stifling in winter. The heat blasts me like steam off the pressing machines as I unlace my boots.

"Don't forget to take your boots off," my father yells from the family room. I'm sure his face is pressed up to the television. I don't think there's a Sunday night game this late in the football season, but he'll be watching ESPN highlights over and over again.

In the kitchen, I grab the cooking spray from the pantry and turn to go back outside.

"Baking cookies out there?" My father startles me as he pushes his way through the swinging doors. He's wearing his standard house uniform: sweatpants, slippers, and a ratty old T-shirt from the Baseball Hall of Fame in Cooperstown. He's had that shirt as long as I can remember. "What do you need cooking spray for?"

I explain how Scott and Jasmine came over to help shovel. Then I tell him about the trick Scott saw on television.

My father shakes his head. Then he goes to the refrigerator and pours himself a soda. "You want one?"

"No thanks. The last thing I need is something cold."

"Tough shoveling, huh?"

He's needling me about the heavy snow, but I don't want to give him the satisfaction.

"Not so bad," I say.

"Not with all the help you recruited. I saw you guys working your way up the side of the house by the family room." He drops a few ice cubes into his drink, and the bubbles fizz up to the lip of the glass, then sink back down. "Jasmine's here, huh?"

"Yeah."

"I didn't think you hung around with her outside of the cleaners."

I want to say, "There's a lot you don't know about me." I want to say, "You're about to learn a hell of a lot more." Those thoughts flash through my mind, but I say nothing.

"You two dating?"

"No." I immediately feel guilty about how fiercely I denied it—like being with Jasmine would be unthinkable. I've stabbed her in the back to please my father. I vow never to do that again.

He pulls back the curtain over the kitchen sink and peers out toward the side of the house. "What, she's dating Scott?"

"No, we're all just friends."

He takes a sip of his soda and leans against the counter.

"Where are you guys off to after this?"

Since when did my father take such an interest in my social life? Almost sixteen years of nothing and now the Spanish Inquisition. "Nowhere. Probably over to Scott's. We have a paper due tomorrow."

"So why the fancy pants, Mr. Fancy Pants?"

I look down and remember I'm wearing Mr. Perry's pants. My winter coat covers the shirt and the leather blazer, but there's no mistaking the creases down the fronts of my legs. There's no mistaking the slacks.

"Everything else is in the hamper," I say.

My father looks me over for a while. His eyes move from my face to my pants three or four times. "Remember, we're doing inventory tomorrow," he says. "We'll get started right after school. Hopefully, I can catch the tail end of practice."

"Sure."

"I'm going to need you to stay late tomorrow night to make calls, too. We have to get people in to pick up their orders. I'm not running a storage facility."

I nod.

"Have fun," he says and disappears back into the family room.

A huge weight lifts off my shoulders. I lace up my boots and gingerly lift Yoko's keys from their hook.

Although we have to reapply it several times, the cooking spray works pretty well. Of course, it doesn't make the snow any lighter, but it's so much easier when the stuff doesn't stick.

We shovel our way up the driveway and around to the back door. Since the driveway wraps around the back of the house, my parents' other two cars won't be in the way. We make a Yoko-width path to the detached garage. Every plunge of my blade into the snow gets me more edgy until finally we are standing right in front of the white garage door.

The lock on the side door of the garage takes the same key

as the front door. I jiggle mine into the knob, and we slip inside. Even in the cold, the smell of motor oil and Armor All is unmistakable. The problem is the automatic garage door. Even I recognize that low rumbling sound from inside the house. If my father hears it going up, he'll come charging out with both guns blaring. Shoot first and ask questions later.

"My mom's got one of these back home in Cincinnati," Scott says, pointing to the motor for the garage door opener. It's like he read my mind. He reaches up and pulls on a yellow cord. It makes a clicking sound. "We can open it manually now. If we do it slowly, no one will hear."

"Once we get the tarp off, we should probably roll it out in neutral," Jasmine says. "We can start it when we get to the street. You sure you still want to do this?"

I clench my teeth and nod.

Scott pulls off the tarp with a single yank.

Even in the darkness of the garage, Yoko gleams. Everything about her is shiny. She's painted deep metallic blue with two wide, white stripes down the hood to the trunk. The polished chrome grille makes her appear to be smiling. It's an impish sort of grin—like she wants to take the trip, too. It's like Yoko is tired of sitting around year after year waiting for perfect weather to take a few laps around the block. She wants to get out there and go on a road trip. And she's daring me to help her.

"You have the keys, right?" Jasmine asks.

I nod.

"Get in," she says. "Put the car in neutral and steer. Scott and I will push. Once we start it up, I'll get in and drive."

"Why don't you just take her out?" I offer.

Jasmine shakes her head. "I don't want to be the one be-hind the wheel when this beauty first leaves her home. You have to do it."

Little does she know we've already taken the first step. For my father, depositing dirty slush on the painted concrete floor of Yoko's garage is like wiping your feet on the kneeling pad in church after stepping in dog shit. My father would no-tice if Yoko was an inch to the left, never mind the havoc we've already caused. He's going to go haywire.

I pop open the driver's door and slide behind the wheel. I'm sure the snow on my boots is melting onto the floor mats.

I grip the steering wheel and close my eyes.

"You okay?" Scott asks. "You look like you're gonna spew chunks."

I nod.

"Put it in neutral then," he says. "Don't make me think this was all a ruse to get us to shovel your driveway."

My hand moves to the shifter, and I clench it in my fist.

"Just slide it down two notches," Jasmine urges.

I lower my head. Despite the icy steering wheel pressing into my forehead, my face is burning. "I can't," I whisper. "I can't do it." I say it over and over again until the words stop making sense in my head. "I can't. I can't. I can't."

Jasmine gets into the passenger seat and slides her hand up my back to my shoulder. "It's okay," she says.

I lift my head and glance at Scott. When my eyes lock on his, he turns around and starts fumbling with the rumpled tarp.

Jasmine squares my shoulders to her and looks into my

eyes. My gaze sinks down. Since she's all twisted in the seat, her dress is riding up on one side. Her legs look great in those panty hose. There's nothing I'd rather do than go with her to the casino, but pulling that shifter down two notches right now seems harder than throwing a cow over the moon. Her fruity smell overpowers the Armor All.

"It's okay," Jasmine says. "We don't have to go."

"I want to. I really do. It's just that—" I feel wet heat brimming around the edges of my eyes.

What's going to happen tomorrow when my father does inventory?

What's he going to do when he finds that money missing?

The proverbial shit is going to hit the proverbial fan.

And now I'm letting down my two closest friends.

I clench my jaw and force the tears to retreat. "Everything's just so screwed up."

Jasmine squeezes my shoulders. "It could be worse," she says.

"Yeah, how?"

She pulls off her gloves. Her bare hand grazes my cheek and makes its way to the side of my face. It feels warm and soft. She puts my earlobe between her fingers and yanks. She yanks hard. Sharp pain rips up my neck into my head.

"Jesus, what the hell did you do that for?" I feel the side of my face for blood, but there's none.

"See? It just got worse."

She's such a goddamn enigma.

"Don't sweat it," Jasmine says. "So, we don't go to the casino tonight. What's the big deal? No pun intended."

I place my hand on hers. "I'll just own up to what I did. My father will have to cope. Call in sick if you don't want to be around."

"Nah, me being there will probably soften the blow."

"Don't count on it."

Jasmine looks down. "Look at you grabbing my hand like that, Casanova."

I feel that vibe and realize I am definitely on the Romantic Response side of my algorithm. Now what do I do?

"I'm just holding it so you can't yank my ear again. Let's cover the car and get out of here."

After we get out of Yoko, Scott throws the tarp over her. I toss a few of the polishing diapers onto the floor and wipe up our footprints on the way out. When I pull the door closed behind me, it makes a hollow thud. At first, I'm afraid my father might hear, but then I remember it doesn't really matter anymore.

HOCKEY STICKS

(two sevens)

My day of reckoning is here. My stomach has been in knots all day, knots that have been tying themselves over and over again in order to find the tightest, most complex snarl possible. The thought of doing inventory at the cleaners makes me want to hunch up and curl into a ball. I can't take my eyes off the classroom clock. Every *tick* of the second hand feels like another step down death row.

And to top it off, I failed another English quiz. How was I supposed to know *Billy Budd* and *Typee* were two different stories? I thought *Typee* was Billy Budd's dog. English is going to be a total bust this marking period. It'll give Mom a reason to disown me after my father kills me.

No matter how hard I've tried to delay the inevitable—lingering in the library, taking the long route to my locker, walking out the front of the school rather than cutting through the gym—I can't avoid it anymore. Each step on my way to work becomes more difficult than the last until I want to run away screaming. I find myself bargaining with some unseen deity.

Just get me out of this and I'll never steal again.

If you make this go away, I'll never look at another playing card my whole life.

Not even Four Horsemen.

If you give me just a few more weeks, I'll put back double the money I took.

Triple.

I stare at the ground and count my footsteps. I pass the post office and the bagel store. I pass the old pencil factory and the abandoned train station. I pass the Chinese restaurant.

Everything is quiet. The piles of snow seem to have swallowed most of the sound. Once I get into a rhythm, the counting calms me down. The numbers are like stepping-stones: firm, unchanging, safe. When I get to a thousand, I look up. The dry cleaners looms before me: the blinking neon sign that the town officials wanted my father to take down, the faded blue poster in the front window that boasts, ONE-HOUR MARTINIZING. Everything about that place makes me cringe. I reach for the door handle.

The door bursts open and smacks into my knuckles. Jasmine rushes past me and darts around the side of the building toward the parking lot. Her head is down, and her shoulders are heaving.

Then I hear my father: "Andrew, get your ass in here!"

I want to chase after Jasmine and find out what happened before I face my father. I want to comfort her, but my father's will pulls me into the stale heat of the dry cleaners.

His cell phone is to his ear, and his face is scarlet.

"Where's Jasmine going?" I ask.

He puts his hand over the receiver. "I knew that girl was trouble from day one." He holds up a finger to silence me and talks into the phone. "Thanks, Betty. Just have him call me when he gets a minute." He snaps the phone shut and clips it to his belt.

"What happened?" *As if I don't already know.*

"Money is missing. A lot of money. I started inventory earlier so I could make it over to the school for practice. The drawer was way short."

The register is askew, and the cash drawer is hanging open.

"I tore this goddamn place apart looking for the missing tickets, and guess what? I found a stack of them hidden neatly under the register. It's the exact amount missing, too. I wasn't born yesterday. That little bitch stole from me. She's out of here. And when Chief McGuire calls me back, I'm going to have her arrested."

I drop my book bag and turn to face him.

"Aside from me and you, she's the only one who's had access to the register." He runs his hands through his hair. "Jesus, what was I thinking hiring a goddamn druggie to work here? I should never have listened to your mother."

"She's not a druggie."

"Yeah?" he says, almost like he's daring me to disagree with him. "Where do you think all that money went? I'll tell you where it went—right up that freak's pierced nose." He points in the direction Jasmine ran off. His hand is shaking.

"It was me," I say. The words explode out of me like a balloon bursting. "I took the money. I took every cent."

My father stares at me with a perplexed look on his face, like the pieces of the puzzle are struggling to find their way together in his mind. He puts a hand on the front counter to steady himself.

"Don't cover up for your little shoveling buddy." He grasps

at the only explanation that would make him right about Jasmine, the only one that would make him right about me.

"I'm telling you, I did it. I gave the customers their clothes, stuck the tickets under the register, and kept the money. Six hundred dollars." I feel a little bigger—a little stronger—when I say it. "Six hundred dollars," I say again. "And it's all gone."

He growls. He sounds just like Jim did when he went after Jasmine.

I feel the slap before I have a chance to roll with it. The pain spreads like a shock through my face. I stagger back but leave my arms down at my sides. I can't say I welcomed the slap, but at some level I feel as though I deserved it.

"How could you steal from me?" my father screams.

He slaps me again. Then he shoves me. My shoulders slam into the corkboard and send the take-out menus flying. "You're stealing your own future." He shoves me and slaps me again. "You're stealing from me, your mother, Rooster." He shoves me into the pay phone. It makes a short *ding* when I smash into it, and the receiver drops from its cradle. The radio on top of the phone teeters but doesn't fall. "You're stealing from your dead grandfather, who worked his whole life to build this business from nothing! I raised you better than this, you little shit!"

"You raised me to be your fucking slave!" Tears stream from my eyes like they've been looking for a way out for a long time.

"Shut your mouth."

"You raised me to work in your store so you could run off to your stupid team!"

"I said shut up!"

He lifts his hand again. This time, I raise my chin to take it, but the blow never comes.

"You think a smack in the face hurts me?" I say. I take a step toward him, but he doesn't back off. We're practically nose to nose. "I'm used to it. Every time you walk out of here wearing your stupid Lady Yellowjackets shirt it's a slap in my face. Every time you leave here you tell me you'd rather hang out with that team of losers than with your own son."

I move toward the door, but my father stands in my way.

"You're staying right here," he says.

"Try and make me." I take another step.

He shoves me again, with both hands this time, and I slam against the counter. I shove him back, and his hands start flailing for anything within reach. I jump away like I've just let a bloodthirsty tiger out of its cage. He throws a stack of receipts at me. They flutter to the ground. He throws a roll of stain stickers at me. It hits the wall to my left. He hurls the stapler at me. He finds his mark. Spikes of pain fire through my whole body.

I put my hand to my forehead and touch where it stings the most. I feel wet heat and look at my fingers. They're covered with traces of glistening red.

"See what you made me do?" he screams. His face is redder and more mottled than I've ever seen it. "Now get in the back and clean yourself up. You're bleeding. We'll talk about this later."

The stapler lies in pieces on the floor.

"Fuck off," I say. It comes out so low and calm I barely recognize my own voice.

And the next thing I know, I'm outside. The cold bites at my stinging forehead.

Jasmine. Where's Jasmine?

I go around the side of the building. She's sitting on the edge of the concrete planter. Her face is buried in her coat sleeve, and her shoulders are shaking.

I hear the front door of the cleaners swing open. "Andrew, get back here!" my father bellows. "We have to talk about this."

He can't see me around the corner, and I stay quiet. After a few seconds, I hear him growl, "Shit!" Then the door slams shut so hard the plate-glass storefront rattles.

I jam my hands into my pockets and walk over to Jasmine. The farther I am from my father and the closer I am to Jasmine, the more relaxed I get. A trickle of blood makes its way to the inner corner of my eye. I blink it away.

"Hey," I say.

She doesn't look up.

"Thanks," I say.

"For what?"

"For not ratting me out."

"No problem." Jasmine looks up at me and squints against the late afternoon sun. "Hey, you're bleeding."

"What is it with us?" My voice is still a little shaky. "One of us is always bleeding."

"I thought you said your father never hits you."

"I guess there's a first time for everything."

She might be smiling but I can't tell; it might be part of her squint. "Jesus," she says. "That job was the only normal part of my life."

"That and scrapbooking."

"Yeah, that and scrapbooking."

A car pulls into the driveway. It's Mrs. Drury with her weekly load of frilly silk blouses. She grabs the bundle of clothes from her backseat and rushes into the building, hardly looking in our direction.

"Got your phone on you?" I ask Jasmine.

"Yeah, why?"

"Call Scott." I rattle off his number.

She keys his number into her cell phone and hits Send. "What's he got, a job for me?"

"He did say you could work at the strip club he wants to open."

"He did not!"

"Just kidding." It's only a small lie. "Tell him to get changed. We're going to the casino after all."

R O U T E   6 6

(two sixes)

Jasmine spins the wheel to the left and hits the gas. Yoko slides around the corner and shoots slush high into the air. Salt sprays all over the sides of the car, and my throat tightens. A voice in my head screams for me to make Jasmine turn around. We can still clean Yoko up and my father will never find out we took her. This car is like religion to him, and we're out here skidding around in the snow.

I tell myself to forget about it. Tonight Yoko is ours. Tonight she's mine.

"Oh, my God," Jasmine says.

"Oh, my God what?" Scott asks from the backseat.

"This car's got some balls."

"No kidding. It's a nineteen seventy Chevelle SS four-fifty-four." I pull my seat belt around me and put my hands near the vent to warm them up. The heater is belching out pure fire. I yank my hands away and tuck them into my jacket pockets. "My father spends a lot of time and money making sure this car runs perfectly. He always brags about how it's one of the fastest muscle cars in history. Of course it's got balls."

"It gets away from you if you're not careful."

"Then be careful," says Scott. "Be extra careful."

We round another corner, and Scott slides across the vinyl seat. He slams into the armrest and grunts.

Jasmine chuckles and rolls past the road that leads to the interstate.

"Where're we going?" I ask her. "The turn for the high-way—"

"I have to get some clothes."

I glance over at her. She's wearing some kind of skirt, black of course, black leggings, and her combat boots. Her peacoat covers everything else.

"You look fine to me."

She angles her body toward me and tugs at the lapel of her coat, exposing her shirt. She's wearing a black tee with white letters that says, NOW THAT I MADE IT OUT, I'M PRO-CHOICE.

Jasmine weaves in and out of a bunch of back streets and pulls into the driveway of a stately house behind a tall row of snow-covered hedges.

"Be right back." She hops out of the car and bolts up the driveway.

Scott pokes his head between the seats. "You think this is *her* house?"

"I guess so. I never asked her where she lives."

"I would've figured Jasmine lived down by the highway or something."

"I'm glad you're so nonjudgmental."

"Since when did you become Mr. Open Mind? Put on some tunes."

I roll the dial from one side to the other, but the radio doesn't pick up anything.

"Is that an eight-track player?" Scott asks, pointing to the center of the black dashboard.

"Yeah. My father put it in aftermarket. I tried to convince him to replace it with a CD player, maybe get an MP3 player in here, but he's holding out for an original radio in mint condition."

"Any eight-tracks around?"

I open the glove compartment. Tucked among the owner's manual, registration, and insurance card is *The Very Best of the Four Seasons*.

"Jeez, that thing is as big as a Kleenex box," Scott says.

"Real high-tech." I plug the cartridge into the player. I can hear the mechanism begin to whir and click. Then the music starts.

"Who'd ever listen to this crap?" Scott says. "The guy sounds like an ambulance siren."

"It's this or static."

Scott throws himself back into his seat. "Give me a few minutes to decide."

Jasmine comes back out of her house clutching a bulky duffel bag. She's wearing the same red dress she had on last night, with killer heels. In the headlights, the dress makes her appear as though she's floating down the driveway. Scott and I already changed at his house. Jasmine gets back in the driver's seat and throws her bag by my feet. It practically crushes my ankles, but I know better than to ask a girl what she's got in her bag.

"All ready," she says. "What is this?" She jabs a finger at the radio.

"It's the Four Seasons," I answer. "It's all we have."

"I guess it's better than a sharp stick in the eye."

"Anyone have a sharp stick?" Scott says.

Jasmine backs out of the driveway, and until we get onto the highway, the car is silent except for the whiny crooning of Frankie Valli, the low growl of the engine, and the hum of the tires on the plowed pavement.

It feels like it was years ago I was pushing my chips "all in" at Shushie's tournament. One mistake after another. But having Jasmine next to me and Scott in the backseat makes it all feel worthwhile. Of course, that doesn't change the fact that I'm dead meat when I get home, but there are definitely worse ways to go.

"Ninety-seven miles," I say, glancing at the directions I printed off the casino website. "An hour and a half."

"Hey," Scott calls from the back. He taps my headrest. "Let me ask you a question."

"Sure."

"If your dad's already caught you, then the cat's out of the bag, right? Why are we still going to the casino?"

I'm about to say I don't know why, that it just feels right, but Jasmine cuts in. "Because we have to. It's like that thing from U.S. history. I forget what it's called when the Americans felt the need to expand out west."

"Manifest Destiny?" I say.

"That's it," Jasmine cries. "Manifest Destiny." She says it like there's a drumroll backing her up.

The road hums under us for a few seconds until Scott finally says, "You do see the irony, don't you?"

I turn around. Scott is lying across the backseat with his head on a rolled-up towel. "What irony?" I say.

"We're going to an *Indian* casino. In the nineteenth century, Americans looked at Manifest Destiny as a chance for expansion and prosperity. But to the Indians, it meant expulsion and genocide."

"You still have those socks in your pocket?"

"Sure." Scott pulls the white athletic socks out.

"Stick them in your mouth."

The tops of the green mile marker signs poke above the surface of the snow. Each one catches our headlights and sends a green flash back at us, as if urging us to keep going. *Green, green, green!* I count them off in my head, and before I know it, we're halfway there.

Jasmine adjusts the rearview mirror, and it distracts me from my counting. "Scott's sleeping," she whispers over the second playing of "Walk Like a Man."

I glance back at him. "When he's out, he's dead to the world. Scott's always been like that."

"Wish I could sleep that well."

"Me too."

My mind scrambles for something to say. The silence is uncomfortable, but it seems harder than ever to think of something to talk about. It's not that I'm afraid I'll sound stupid. It's more like I feel I need to say something meaningful and important. I'm on the right branch of my algorithm. It's all new territory for me. Finally, I take the leap—and it's a big one.

"Have you spoken to Jim?"

There's a long pause. Then she changes the subject. "What do you think will happen if we get caught?"

"*When* we get caught," I say.

"Remember when Anthony Prudente got nailed up at the lake with his father's Blazer? The family court judge sent him to some state youth facility."

I can't imagine what it would be like going to a youth facility. I've seen them in movies and everything, but it's the first time the thought of being in one myself has entered my mind. "Yeah, but Prudente had all sorts of trouble before that— some vandalism stuff and breaking into a hardware store and that one time he slashed all the school bus tires."

"I guess so."

"Anyhow, if we get pulled over, I'll take the blame," I say.

"You're taking a lot of that lately."

I shrug, and we let a few minutes pass in silence until I finally push the issue. "So, you didn't answer my question about Jim."

Jasmine exhales through her nose. "I called him earlier— on my cell phone—after I got fired. I told him what happened and that I wanted to see him."

"Jasmine." I hate to lecture her, but I can't help myself. "You have to stay away from that guy."

"I didn't have anyone else to call, all right? Anyhow, why do you think I agreed to come on this trip? I knew the best thing was to get away from him—to go with you."

"Well, at least you're coming to your senses," I say.

"I didn't know you had such a high opinion of yourself."

"No, I mean you finally figured out that it's better to break around twenty laws than to hang out with that asshole."

My hand makes its way to Jasmine's knee, where I find her

hand. She turns her hand over and squeezes mine back. Her skin is soft, and I want to raise her fingers to my lips. But I don't.

Before long, the light from the approaching hotel fills the misty sky above clusters of dark trees and the casino comes into full view. I've seen pictures of this place on television commercials, but it looks much larger in real life. The hotel soars into the air at least thirty stories, and another tower is under construction. Each blue neon letter on the front of the building is bigger than a house, and the parking lot is so sprawling there are shuttle buses to pick you up at your car. Seeing the casino in full view sets me on edge. Deep inside me, fear is battling with excitement.

And fear is quickly losing.

H I L T O N   S I S T E R S

(two queens)

Despite the shrill music drilling into my brain the whole car ride, I can't get Sinatra's "Luck Be a Lady" out of my head. Shushie would always play that song at the club when he decided to sit in on a game. Jasmine, Scott, and I stride toward the casino, and I wonder if I'm feeling the same excitement a mouse feels just before he reaches for the cheese on the mousetrap. We make our way through the first set of automatic doors, and I notice how perfectly clean the lobby is. Not even my doctor's office is this pristine.

Huge green and beige swirls spread across the burgundy carpet. It reminds me of Medusa's hairdo. I find myself walking along the curves of the design rather than in a straight line toward the gaming room. In fact, when I look around, I realize there are very few straight lines in the whole place, as though the casino wraps around the curve of the earth.

"You sure about this?" Scott asks through the side of his mouth.

"Just shut up and walk," Jasmine says. "Try to look confident—like you belong here."

"That's easy for you to say," Scott hisses. "You guys could pass for my parents."

"Stop talking out of the side of your mouth," I say. "Do you *want* them to card us? Just act normal."

People always tell me I look mature for my age. It must be something in my jawline or how my eyes are deep-set like my mother's. But I've never been more self-conscious about my appearance than right now. *Does my hair look too boy band? Am I walking like a kid or a man? Should I swing my arms more?* I'm not that much younger than the legal limit here—you only have to be eighteen to play—but if they ask me for identification, I'm dead in the water.

We leave our winter jackets in the coatroom. Jasmine checks her bag, too.

I watch her stride a few paces ahead of me. She could easily pass for twenty-five. And I mean that as a compliment. She's curvy and confident and wears a lot of makeup. In her heels, she marches through the inner set of automatic doors like she owns the place—like she's the proprietor of the whole damn casino.

Scott, on the other hand, is a problem. He definitely looks sixteen. Maybe younger. With his oily complexion, he could never be mistaken for anything but a teenager. It's worth the risk, though. He's the one with the sock full of money.

At the wide archway into the casino, a solitary guard stands posted with his hands clasped behind his back. His blue, short-sleeved uniform shirt stretches tight across his paunch. If it weren't for the mustache clinging for life to his upper lip, he would look as young as Scott. His eyes remain fixed on the floor and turned toward the side of the corridor. It's as though he doesn't *want* to see us. I'm sure he'll swing his gaze in our direction any moment and demand to see our licenses. I only have my permit, and Scott's never bothered at all.

We continue to walk.

The guard lifts his fist to his mouth and clears his throat.

We continue to walk.

My eyes stay fixed on the guard, but I keep my head facing forward.

The security guard shifts his weight to his other foot. He clears his throat again, this time louder.

Did he clear his throat to get our attention? Did he call us over?

I decide to ignore him, and we breeze right past into the chaos of the casino. Going into the gaming area feels like entering another world. The whole place, with its stuffed wolves and neon dream catchers, looks like the American Museum of Natural History in New York City if it were overhauled by Disney.

"That was close," Scott says.

"Close?" I say. "The guy barely noticed us."

"Didn't you hear him cough? He was trying to get our attention."

"Right, and if he scratched his ass you'd say he was reaching for his cuffs."

"Both of you shut up," Jasmine says. "Let's get into the middle of everything, away from the guards."

The casino is huge. Really huge. Cavernous. I don't think I've ever been in a larger room. It's bigger than the school gym. It's bigger than ten school gyms. There are pillars all over the place, but the ceiling still seems to defy gravity. The constant ringing and beeping of slot machines assaults me. *Listen to all the people winning. Listen to all the people whose lives are changing.* My hand glides to my pocket, and I realize Scott is still holding most of the money.

Jasmine thrusts a large plastic cup into my hands. It has the casino name, CRYSTAL WATERS CASINO, in ice blue letters superimposed over a bubbling waterfall. The orange-red lighting makes Jasmine's pale skin glow.

"Hang on to this," she says. She hands a cup to Scott, too.

"How come?" I say. "I'm playing poker."

"It'll make the security guards think you've been gambling already. They won't question you because they'll figure some other guard already did."

"Good idea," Scott says.

"And if security comes up to you," she adds, "tell them you're looking for your parents."

"I have to get some change," Scott says. "I want to put some money in those slots." The lighting makes him look ruddier than my great-aunt Margaret at her wake when I was seven. Flo, one of Aunt Maggie's bridge partners, said she looked like a painted whore. On the ride home, I asked my mom what *whore* meant, but all I got was a grunt from my father.

We make our way through a maze of slot machines. Hundreds of little old ladies, cigarettes pinched between pursed lips, work three or more machines at once. Each one eyes me suspiciously, as if I might try to edge in on her territory.

The jackpot numbers creep up, up, up, and I find myself wanting to feed money into the machines, too. But slot machines are not my thing. I can't understand people who drop quarter after quarter—dollar after dollar—into a machine that is programmed to pay you back at a cut rate. I did a lot of reading about different casino games on the Internet. You may as well flush seven cents of every dollar down the toilet. Even blackjack is stacked in the casino's favor. If you play a perfect game, statistics say you'll lose a few cents on every dollar you spend. Sure, you can have a good day every so often—that's what gambling is all about—but over time you'll lose.

With poker, my success depends on me alone. How much I win depends upon the decisions I make about my hand and what I can learn about the other players at the table. Of course, the house gets its cut, a few dollars every hand, but if I can outplay one or two of the other players at the table, I can clean up. My destiny is in my own hands.

Countless signs hang from the ceiling and point in every direction—to every game, every buffet, every restaurant, and every store in the place. It's like a playground—no, an amusement park—for adults. I follow the arrow that points to the poker room. It leads me through a huge field of gaming tables. Jasmine and Scott trail behind me.

We walk straight past the gaming tables; I only get a moment to glance at each one. The blackjack dealers deal cards with calm efficiency to a sea of people. The craps tables have a carnival feel to them, with people jumping and screaming like they're on the floor of the stock exchange. Old guys with dark hats and chewed-up cigars surround the roulette tables. The exhaust fans whisk the smoke straight up and out through the vents. There are plenty of games I've never heard of: Pai Gow, Let It Ride, Caribbean Stud. They even play War here. I breeze through the gaming area, barely glancing at any of them.

If I had the time, I'd watch each game for an hour, but every moment I waste is a Hold 'Em hand missed. I need to play poker.

I almost walk past the poker room, but Scott grabs my jacket. "Dude, it's right there." He points to a large, bright area behind a row of glass partitions. The words CRYSTAL WATERS CASINO POKER ROOM are etched into the glass. Silent televisions airing sporting events hang from brackets in every free spot, and No Smoking signs are posted everywhere. There are about fifty tables, each with a bow-tie-wearing dealer and an automatic card-shuffling machine. Waitresses wiggle their way between the tables, trays in hand, like those cigar girls you see in old movies. The room is quieter than the rest of the casino, the only sounds being hushed murmurs and the click of chips.

I knew the employees wouldn't be wearing feather headdresses and moccasins, but I expected them to look Native American in some way—dark skin, high cheekbones, whatever. But every dealer, every waitress—every employee—is whiter than Wonder Bread, like every trailer park in a fifty-mile radius sent their best and brightest.

Definitely not what I expected.

"Scott and I will wait here," Jasmine says to me. "Go in and get a seat."

"No," Scott protests. "I want to go up to the desk with Andrew."

"What are you, two years old?" Jasmine says to Scott. "You want him to get carded?"

Scott shoves his hands in his pockets and turns away.

I squeeze Jasmine's arm and walk into the poker room alone.

Just like in Shushie's club, a huge dry erase board hangs behind a desk on the back wall. The board lists all the games, their limits, and how many seats are available at each table, along with the names of people waiting to play each game. The wait for the $3–$6 Texas Hold 'Em table seems short. It's a good place for me to start—you can't lose too much too fast. I step up to the counter.

A middle-aged woman, obviously the poker room manager, smiles at me. Two older men wearing suits flank her. Her name tag says AMELIA, and she's wearing thick, black glasses attached to a cord that loops around her neck. Her graying blond hair is pulled up in a clip, but a few stray curls trail down her forehead. "What can I do for you, sugar?" she says. I didn't expect a southern accent at an Indian casino. Her left eye looks as though the iris leaked into the white part, like if you were to stab at a sunny-side-up egg with a fork.

I try not to stare, but I know I already am. My gaze shifts down to the desktop, and I grab a brochure for the casino and a calendar of upcoming tournaments. I stuff them in my inside pocket, my secret agent pocket, and try to talk to her again without staring at her shriveled-up eye.

"I'd like a seat at a three–six Hold 'Em table, please."

"Do you have a poker room membership card?"

"A what?"

"A membership card." She points at the cashier window. "You need to get a membership card to play. It's five hundred dollars for the night."

"Five hundred dollars?" My voice almost cracks, but I manage to keep it under control.

"I'm just pulling your leg, sugar." The two men behind Amelia chuckle as though they've heard the same gag hundreds of times. "It's only five dollars. I like to have a little fun with you newcomers."

With a smile, I head over to the window. I pull out my hundred-dollar bill and slide it through the bars. "I'll take a membership card and the rest in chips."

Another woman, who seems more like a robot than a human, waves my bill under a purple light and places it faceup on the countertop. She stamps a small, white card with the time and date. Then she lifts a Lucite chip carrier loaded with white chips from a stack, removes five chips, and slides the carrier and membership card to me through the grating. The money disappears into the cash drawer.

"Good luck," she says.

I go back to Amelia with my card. One of the older men wearing a suit asks me my name, and I say the first lie that pops into my head. "Chip."

A knowing smile spreads across Amelia's face. "We get a lot of 'Chips' here."

The man writes "Chip" at the bottom of the $3–$6 Hold 'Em column. "Listen for your name," he says. "Don't go far. If you don't come up right away, we have to give your seat to the next person on the list."

"Will I be able to hear my name out there?" I point beyond the glass partition where Jasmine and Scott are waiting.

"Sure, sugar," Amelia says. "You'll be able to hear it all the way to the first row of blackjack tables. If you keep those cute little ears of yours perked up, you might be able to hear it out by keno."

I say thanks and make my way out of the poker room, scanning the tables for any familiar faces from Shushie's. I'm relieved to see none.

"What happens now?" Scott asks.

"As soon as a seat opens up, I go back in and sit down. Once I do, I can stay as long as I like. I signed up for a three–six—a low-limit game."

"How long you think it'll be?" Scott asks. He stands way too close. I can feel his breath on me as he talks. I take a step back.

"Not long."

Scott takes the rolled-up socks out of his pocket and un-wraps his money. "I have three fifty." He counts out two hun-dred dollars in fives and tens and stuffs them in my hand. "The rest is for Jasmine and me."

"I have my own money," Jasmine says.

"You better save it," I say. "You're unemployed."

"So are most of the other people here."

As Jasmine and Scott walk off, I watch Jasmine's hips sway back and forth. They disappear into the labyrinth of blinking machines, and I decide to follow them. Scott fills his plastic cup with change, and we find a few machines next to each other. I figure playing the slots for a few minutes is better than standing around with my head up my ass.

There's something about the beeping, blinking, and spin-ning of the slot machine wheels that sucks me in. I never ex-pected it, but it's like playing FreeCell on the computer. If I lose, I want to play until I win. If I win, I want to keep the streak going. *Once more, once more, once more,* I keep saying to myself as I hit the Spin button over and over. We're only playing quarter machines, so even if we do hit it big, we won't score too much. Jasmine hits for forty credits, ten dollars, and she goes bananas.

After about twenty minutes, Scott nudges me. "Did I see them write the name Chip on the board when you went over there?"

"Yeah." I never give my real name, not even at Shushie's. I don't like it up there for everyone to see. "How come?"

"They just called you on the speaker."

My head swivels around, and I dart toward the poker room. "Someone take my machine," I call over my shoulder. "There are twelve credits left in there."

As soon as I pass the glass partition, Amelia waves to me. "Over there, sugar," she says and motions to a table set off in the corner. I glance down at the Lucite rack almost filled with white chips. Ninety-five dollars. My hand goes to the two hundred in my pocket, and I make my way over to Amelia.

"Can I get a seat at a ten–twenty Hold 'Em table instead?" I ask her.

She glances at the dry erase board. "Sure, we have a few seats open. Table seventeen." She points at a table not far from the entrance. "Good luck, sugar."

I take the only available seat at Table 17. It's toward the end of the oblong table, diagonal from the dealer. It's a good spot because I can see the dealer's face and still get a good look at just about everyone else playing.

A twelve-hand game means I'll have to play tight. The more people at the table, the more selective you need to be about playing a hand. Even in good position, I won't jump in on anything worse than a queen-nine off suit.

I'm greeted with a flurry of welcoming smiles and nods, and I stack my chips in front of me. The heavy guy sitting to my right, a man wearing really strong cologne, tells me in a raspy voice to toss the chip carrier under the table. I do.

I push my white chips to the dealer and ask for all fives. Then I slide the bills Scott gave me across the table and ask the dealer for an additional two hundred.

I think about what Amelia said to me—*Good luck, sugar*—and I realize that's why she's on the other side of the desk collecting a meager paycheck instead of playing out here with us. This game has nothing to do with luck.

I place two chips in front of me and wait for my first two cards.

BIG SLICK

(a king and an ace)

The dealer, whose name tag says RUDY, sits on a swivel chair raised up all the way. Rudy's arms are really short. So short, in fact, that I can't imagine how he decided to take up card dealing as a career. He can deal though. He can deal really well.

I always wonder how dealers do it. It amazes me how they flawlessly fire out hand after hand, calculate split pots, and keep the game running smoothly without making mistakes every second. I would totally choke if I tried to do it. All those people with all that money at stake. Arguments break out all the time. The stress levels can get pretty brutal.

I glance at the eleven other players sitting around the table. I have to start making books on them—figuring out how each player plays the game, if they're aggressive or conservative, loose or tight. Knowing how someone plays is a huge advantage. It's why Internet poker is so lame. You can't see your opponents' body language. Not to mention if there's no real money at stake, people tend to bet recklessly.

The guy to my right, the one with the cologne, leans toward me and extends his hand. I shake it, but he pumps four or five times more than I'm comfortable with. And really hard. "Nice to meet you," he says. "Harris Macklin."

"Chip," I say. "Chip Churchill." I don't know where I came up with that name. It just popped into my head.

"Chip. Is that short for Charles?"

"Thanks to Grandpa." My grandfather's name was Max, but the lies keep pouring from my mouth.

Harris leans back in his seat. A fresh wave of cologne stench washes over me, like there was a repository of it hidden underneath one of his fat rolls. He exhales through his nose, and his breath slips over my forearm. I move my hand to my lap.

"I hope you have better luck than me tonight," he says. "These dealers have been sending me crap for hours."

I study the other players. Starting to Rudy's left, there's Polo (for his blue striped shirt), Caterpillar (from the unibrow over his eyes), Blondie (for the mess of hair peeking out from under her baseball cap), Gold (from the dozen or so chains and pendants around her neck), Roker (for his likeness to the weatherman Al Roker), and Nose (for obvious reasons). Then there's Harris, then me. To my left are Flying Squirrel (her skin is so crinkly and saggy that she could glide on the wind if she spread her arms out), Bourbon (for the bottle of Jack Daniel's he keeps by his feet), Lamppost (from how skinny he is), and Cleavage (for her low-cut sweater).

"Good luck, Boo," Gold says. I look up at her, unsure if she's talking to me. Her hair is stringy and greasy, as though she hasn't taken a shower in a week, and her face is the color of a filled-up ashtray.

"Chip," I say.

"What's that?" She leans forward, and one of her pendants clinks against the lip of her soda glass.

"Chip. My name's Chip."

She brushes her hand in the air as though she's sweeping my words into the trash. "I call everyone Boo. If I really like you, I'll call you Boo-Boo."

"Well, by the end of the night, I hope you're calling me Boo-Boo."

She smiles. Her teeth all angle inward like two rows of the highway tire spikes I've seen the cops use on television. "You're well on your way." Her gaze shifts to my forehead. "Oh, Boo, what happened?"

Everyone's head—even Rudy's—swivels toward me. They all give my wound the once-over and then get back to whatever it was they were doing.

My fingers find their way to the lump I got from my father's stapler. It aches when I press it, and I can feel a rough scab. "You should see the other guy."

"Chip doesn't want to talk about that," Harris says, wrapping an arm around my shoulders. "He came here to play some poker."

I stack my chips in six neat piles and look at my first hand—a two and a three off suit. I fold. The next few hands come, and they're all junk. I fold them, too.

Rudy's short arms are a real disadvantage. He has trouble reaching across the table to scoop up cards or pull chips into the pot. Every once in a while, I leave my cards just out of reach so he has to lean all the way forward. Seeing Rudy's ass lift off the seat cracks me up.

Just like Harris said, Rudy keeps dealing me garbage. The button travels a full circuit around the table, and I fold every hand. Sixteen hands pass me by—all crap. After that, a few playable ones come my way. Some I win; some I fold. My biggest loss is $50 (to Roker). My biggest win is $135 (from Bourbon, Lamppost, and Blondie). After three hours, I'm up nearly $500.

People see poker on television and think it's all about energy and excitement, guts and glory. That might be true with a no-limit game, which is like a crazy, out-of-control roller coaster—people bust or double up every few minutes. Limit games, on the other hand, where serious players make their money, are slow, long grinds. The true test is of stamina—how many times a player can fold until a playable hand comes along.

Most people get frustrated by all the bad starting hands. They start to jump in on the bad ones just to get a little action. I used to do that. Now I look at folding as an opportunity to watch the other players at the table. I like to get a feel for them. Half the fun is making my book.

Polo thinks he's hot shit. He acts like every hand is the last hand at the World Series of Poker. And he gets really steamed if he loses. His whole head gets red. When he gives up even an ante, he lectures the other players on why they should have folded before him.

Caterpillar and Blondie are together, like boyfriend and girlfriend. They lean toward each other and get all kissy-kissy between hands. The most they ever bet against each other is a raise or two, then Blondie gets out of Caterpillar's way.

Gold has no idea what she's doing. She plays marginal hands to the hilt and is burning through her stack fast. It's like she's playing with someone else's money. If I see an opportunity, I'll have to bet into her even if it does jeopardize my chances of being promoted to Boo-Boo.

Roker and Nose are tight players and don't talk too much. When they play a hand, it's because they have good cards. I challenge them only when I have very promising starting cards.

Harris's problem is that he flashes me almost every hand. He tries to conceal his cards by putting both hands over them, but he extends his arms all the way out and turns the corners up too high. We're so packed around the table that his hands are right in my line of sight. I see what he's holding every time. Harris whistles, too. I start thinking it might be one of his tells. He seems to whistle only when he's holding decent cards. He tried to bluff once—he was holding a nine and a seven of clubs. Shit cards. Not a sound escaped his lips. I tell myself to keep my eye on the whistling.

Flying Squirrel seems more concerned about her friends hogging the slots on the other side of the glass partition than about keeping her eyes on the game. Her stack is slowly disappearing. I find out she's on a cross-country tour from Portland, Oregon. I also find out she's never played poker outside the senior center before. My biggest fear with her has nothing to do with cards; it's getting slapped in the head with her arm flab.

Cleavage knows the dealer. She talks to him between hands. I figure she either works here or comes here all the time. In any event, she probably knows a lot about cards. I tell myself to watch out for her.

I peek at my next hand—ace of hearts and king of spades.

A king and ace in the hole are called Big Slick. It's "Big" because it's a huge starting hand, one of the best possible. It's "Slick" because it can quickly lead to a terrible hand if the right cards don't come on the flop. Harris, who I see is holding a seven-nine off suit and is not whistling, is the big blind. So I'm the first to act this round.

"Raise," I say. I place four chips in front of me. It's a twenty-dollar bet, ten to call the blind and ten to raise.

Betting with the blinds just to my right tells the other players that I'm either sitting on a big starting hand or trying to steal the antes. If this were a no-limit game, I might steal the antes with a huge bet, but since the raise is restricted to ten dollars, I know someone else is going to call. There are eleven other players; one of them is bound to have a playable starting hand. And being that my hand might turn to crap after the flop, I have to be careful not to get sucked in too deep.

Flying Squirrel and Bourbon fold. Lamppost calls, his veiny hands creeping over the felt. Cleavage, Polo, Caterpillar, and Blondie fold. Gold raises another ten dollars. Roker and Nose fold. Harris, the big blind, calls. The betting has to travel around the table again until it gets back to the last person to raise. Everyone calls. When the betting is done, it's Harris, me, Lamppost, and Gold, with $125 in the pot.

Rudy deals the flop. Two of spades, five of diamonds, and six of diamonds. None of it helps me, but it probably doesn't help anyone else either. A two, five, and six are lower than most players would stay in on, so it's not likely anyone paired up. The only danger to me is a pocket pair or maybe two diamonds in the hole. I remind myself not to rule out Gold staying in on awful cards.

Harris checks.

I do the same.

Lamppost and Gold check, too.

That's a good sign. Chances are I've still got the best hand.

Rudy deals the next card. It's a king of hearts. I leave my eyes on the card and concentrate on remaining still. That king gives me a pair with an ace kicker just in time for the higher betting rounds. In a $10–$20 game, the first two rounds of betting are limited to ten dollars, but for the rest of the hand the limit goes up to twenty.

Harris checks.

I place a twenty-dollar bet in front of me.

Lamppost calls. He's going along for the ride, calling every bet; he's waiting on something, maybe that diamond flush, and trying to get it as cheap as possible.

"I like that action, Boo." Gold raises another twenty, but I know she's reckless. Just because she's reckless doesn't mean she has bad cards, but I'm confident I'm in a better position than she is.

"I'm not gonna chase this one down," Harris says. He tosses his cards in.

I raise again. This poker room, like most casinos, has a three-raise maximum, so that's it for the round.

Lamppost calls and Gold calls.

With the last card coming, we're sitting on about a three-hundred-dollar pot. Not bad on the turn for a $10–$20 table.

Rudy peels another card off the deck with his stubby fingers and turns it up. It's a ten of spades. It makes me just a little nervous. I was hoping for an ace or a king, which would bolster my hand, or something really low. Now, if Gold is holding a king and a ten, she'll have me beat with two pairs to my one.

Lamppost's shoulders, which look like he has a wire coat hanger jammed under his shirt, sag, and I know he was waiting for another diamond. He was holding two, and with two more on the board, he was hoping for the flush. His spindly fingers move to his cards, and I can see he's ready to toss them in.

And he does, even before I get my twenty-dollar bet out in front of me.

"What are you holding over there, Boo?" Gold licks her lips and stares at me for a second. I know she's going to call. She's already done this a few times. She's going to want to keep me honest—to make sure I'm holding something. Now that all the cards have been dealt, there's no chance involved. The cards are what they are. Even if she's holding crap, it will only cost her another twenty dollars to see what I've got. If she doesn't call, I don't need to show. Calling is a losing move on her part, but a lot of people can't stand not knowing what they lost to. Curiosity overrides good sense.

Gold pushes the four five-dollar chips out. "Whatcha got?"

I turn over my ace and king. She smiles her hazardous-looking smile and flips over her cards. King of diamonds and jack of clubs. We both have pairs of kings, but I have the ace kicker. "Take it, Boo," she says.

I toss my cards to the center and scoop up my chips. I start stacking them in piles of ten. And all at once I go from around eight hundred dollars to over a thousand.

I hear a single person clapping behind me. It's Jasmine.

She's holding her empty casino cup between her forearm and chest. I wave to her. She waves back and walks over.

"Hey," she says.

"What's up?"

"I don't know. I've been watching you for a few minutes. Poker looks boring."

"I used to think that until I started playing. Poker kicks ass."

"Maybe for you math geniuses."

Gold claps her hands. "You said it!" She elbows Roker in the arm. "You hear that, Boo? That gal said I'm a math genius."

Roker squeezes out a smile and peeks at his next hand.

When my turn comes, I fold my jack-two off suit.

"What's up?" I ask Jasmine.

"Me? I lost at the slots."

"All of it?"

"And some of Scott's."

"What's he up to?" I say.

"You wouldn't believe it if I told you."

"Try me."

Jasmine squats next to me and puts her hand on my shoulder. She tucks her head between Harris and me. I can see right down the front of her dress, and she makes no move to conceal herself. "A few minutes after you ran in here to grab your seat at the poker table, some woman sat down at the machine next to Scott. I'm not talking some girl. I mean some woman; she must've been like forty or something. At first she was just chatting with him, but soon they were flirting like hell. She's asking him all about himself and he's lying up a storm, telling her he's home on Christmas break from Columbia and that I'm his second cousin from Peoria. Peoria? Where the hell did he get that?"

"Woo hoo!" Gold howls. "Your buddy's getting lucky tonight." She elbows Roker again. "You hear that, Boo? And us just sitting here wasting the night away around a poker table."

Roker shakes his head and buries his chin in his chest.

Jasmine smirks at Gold and continues in a softer voice. "Anyway, the woman gets up and says, 'I want you to have this,' with this really funny look in her eyes. She hands Scott her casino cup filled halfway up with quarters. Then she turns around and takes off. There must have been fifty dollars in that cup. Maybe more."

"Weird," I say.

"Weird's right. Wait until you hear what happened next."

"You're up," Bourbon says, pointing to the cards in front of me. He seems pretty bombed now. His eyes are all glassy, and he's slouching in his seat.

I peek at my hand. Ten-four off suit. I fold.

"Anyhow," Jasmine says, "he held on to the lady's cup, figuring she just went to the bathroom or something. After around twenty minutes, he took a few laps around the casino to look for her. He figured maybe she forgot about her money."

"Then what happened?" asks Gold. Even though everyone's still playing, they're all listening to Jasmine's story, too.

"Finally, Scott decides we should start playing with the lady's money. He drags me to the other side of the casino in case she comes back, and we start feeding the Sahara Special machines."

"What, did he hit big?" It's something I've been afraid of since the drive out here. If any of us hits a big jackpot, we're in trouble. When the sirens go off and the money pours out of the machine, the casino manager comes over and makes you fill out tax forms and show ID and everything. I saw it on a television show about Vegas once.

"I'd say he hit big. The cup was between us, and we were both dipping in for quarters when finally I felt something at the bottom."

"What was it?"

"Yeah, what was it, Boo?"

Jasmine shoots a let-me-finish look over at Gold and starts addressing the whole table instead of just me.

"It was one of those electronic key cards," Jasmine says. "She left her room key in the cup."

A chuckle spreads around the table.

Flying Squirrel puts her hand on her chest. "Oh, lordy!" she says.

"At least someone's getting some action tonight," Gold says.

"Room numbers aren't printed on those keys," I say.

"I know that," Jasmine says. "And Scott knew it, too. We figured the lady probably dropped the key in there by accident, so we kept playing until all the quarters were gone. We were about to chuck the cup—and the key—when a slip of paper fell out. It must have been flat at the bottom. The paper had the room number written right on it with, get this, a lipstick print."

The whole table erupts in a roar of laughter.

"Scott wasn't stupid enough to go up there, was he?" I say. Jasmine levels her eyes to mine, and I realize Scott's stupid enough to do much worse.

"What should we do?" I ask her.

"Aw, let him have his fun, Boo," Gold says in her raspy smoker's voice. "You can come up to my room if you feel left out."

Jasmine shakes her head and shrugs. "Nothing we can do, I suppose. I don't even know what room he went to. Six something."

I look at my watch. It's ten-thirty. My father must have found out about Yoko by now. I left the garage door wide open. There's no way he could have missed it. I wonder briefly if he's called the police, but I don't feel nearly as bad as I thought I would.

"What do you want to do?" I ask Jasmine. "I have two comps for the steak house."

"What's a comp?"

"A freebie the casino gives you if you play long enough."

"I'm not really hungry," she says. "I have a better idea, but finish up first."

That's another cool thing about Jasmine. Most girls would be whining to go by now or asking for more money to play the slots, but she tells me to take my time. She's happy just hanging out. She's happy that I'm happy. I play until the button comes around once more. I pick up another $115—mostly from Polo, who blows a gasket and tells me I should have folded my queen-jack after the flop. It makes me want to keep playing. But when I look over at Jasmine in Mrs. Bonneau's short, red dress, I realize I'd rather be with her. I say my good-byes, tip Rudy $20, and stack my chips into several Lucite racks I find scattered on the floor.

"Toodles, Boo-Boo," Gold says with a wave. "Come on back later and let me win my money back."

If I came back later and by some stroke of luck she had any chips left, I could take her down in no time. I smile at Gold and make my way across the poker room. I cash out at the window and stuff the bills into my pocket. After I separate out Scott's money, my winnings total $1,255. All profit.

We swing by the coat check, and Jasmine gets her duffel bag. Then she leads me to the elevator and presses the Up button.

When I show Jasmine the cash I won, her eyes light up. "Holy moly," she says. "You've made more than enough to pay your father back."

"What's it matter at this point? I'm already busted."

"You need to pay him back. You stole from him."

I get a sinking feeling, as though we were already on the elevator, and I know she's right. I will pay my father back. I'll pay him back and more.

As soon as the door opens, Jasmine grabs my arm and pulls me in.

"Where're we going?" I ask.

"It's a surprise." She presses the button for the top floor, and up we go.

PROM NIGHT
(a suited six and nine)

When I step onto the elevator, I realize it's one of those glass-and-chrome numbers that has all sorts of sparkly white lights around the edges. As we go up, the casino floor sinks from view. Just like my mom, I've never been very good with heights, and I find myself stepping back toward the solid door.

"What's the matter?" Jasmine asks. "Scared or something?"

"No."

"Well, don't worry," she says, grabbing my arm with both hands. "I'll protect you from the big, bad elevator."

The ride seems to take forever, but I don't mind with Jasmine holding on to me. Her touch makes my arm tingle all the way to my fingertips. The elevator comes to a stop, and we get out into a hallway that smells like chlorine. The carpet is green and thin, like the one in the entrance hall to the YMCA where my father coaches basketball during summer leagues.

Jasmine leads me down the hall until we reach a thick glass door. The room on the other side of the door is dim, lit only by the neon railings that line the roof of the casino. The lighting gives the place an eerie blue glow, but there's enough light to see a swimming pool enclosed by four greenhouse-type walls—an indoor rooftop pool.

"I came up here after Scott disappeared." Jasmine leans against the door, and it swings open. "It closed at nine, but it's not locked." She darts into the room and starts wriggling out of her clothes as she makes her way across the blue tile. She flings her dress and shoes aside but gets hung up on her panty hose, doing a funny hopping dance on one leg. Finally, she dives into the pool wearing only her panties and bra. Even though it's dark and shadowy, I study every curve on her body as if there's going to be a section about her on the SATs.

When she surfaces, she turns around, and my gaze drops to the tile. A mosaic of an eagle spans the floor like a huge, immovable carpet.

"Come on in," Jasmine says. "I'll give you a swimming lesson."

Her voice echoes off the walls so loud, I expect the Crystal Waters Hotel and Casino Rooftop Pool Police to come charging in, billy clubs in hand. I glance back down the hallway, but the pool is the only thing up here. We're completely alone.

I arrange Jasmine's clothes neatly on the patio table next to her duffel bag. I suppose keeping clothes clean and neat is in my blood. Plus, Mrs. Bonneau would surely flip out if she got her dress back and it had chlorine stains all over it. Sitting on one of the recliners, I start to unlace my shoes. I take each one off, followed by my socks. I do it slowly, hoping Jasmine will become distracted by something so I can get undressed without her staring at me, especially considering the bulge growing in my pants. Even with my underwear on, there's no hiding where all my blood is rushing. But Jasmine swims over and rests her forearms on the lip of the pool.

"What, are you shy? Underwear is the same as a swimsuit."

Logic tells me she's right, but *my* equipment is on the outside.

I take off my shirt and get a little self-conscious about how skinny I am. Okay, I get a lot self-conscious. I have no chest, no arms. I'm more like a boy than anything else—maybe some kind of boy-guy hybrid. When I get down to my boxer briefs, I have to shift gears so I don't look like a walking coat hook. I head straight for the water and dive over Jasmine's head. The quicker I get in, the less time she'll have to wonder what she's doing with a scrawny, overexcited kid like me.

The water is warm—much warmer than the winter air that penetrates the huge panes of glass. The pool must be heated.

As I surface, I feel Jasmine swimming up behind me. She tugs on my foot, and her head pokes up next to mine. Her mascara sends black rivulets down her face that branch into dozens of tributaries. She grabs my head and pulls my lips to hers. I suck in a deep breath through my nose and flail my feet until they find the tile at the bottom of the pool.

I put my arms around her and pull her close. We seem to fit together perfectly, like two jigsaw puzzle pieces. Her skin is slick under my fingers, interrupted only by her bra strap. Her tongue barbell clicks against my teeth, but this time I'm ready for it. I open my mouth wider.

In no time, Jasmine pushes me to the pool steps, where I sit. She straddles my legs. I let my hands roam over her thighs and her sides. It takes a few minutes for me to get up the nerve to let them go anywhere else. But eventually they do.

When it comes to girls, I'm pretty inexperienced—okay, totally inexperienced. I'm surprised by what breasts feel like. I'd always imagined they'd be taut and springy, like water balloons, but they're softer, more forgiving, like uncooked chicken. Actually, that's a bad comparison. If uncooked chicken felt this amazing, every guy would hang out in the Purdue section at the supermarket.

Jasmine unhooks her bra and lets it drift away on the surface of the water.

All I can do is stare.

Jasmine looks down at me. Her eyes narrow so her dark mascara swallows her eyeballs. "You look like you've never seen a half-naked girl before."

"I guess that's because I haven't—not for real."

She smiles. "That's cute."

Cute. I don't know if I like *cute*, but it's definitely better than *gross* or *go away*. I lower my head to her skin and plant kisses down her neck and along her collarbone. For the first time, I can taste the sweetness I've craved for so long. She responds with tiny squirms punctuated by soft moans that urge me on. I want to devour every last bit of her.

Light filters into the dark room and makes her skin seem pinker than usual. Pink. Jasmine pink. She's usually as pale as baby powder.

We continue kissing and groping for a while—I'm not sure for how long. Time seems to work differently when there's a girl straddling your legs. But we keep going at it until she slides off my lap and wriggles her hand into the waistband of my underwear.

I once read in a trivia book that it is impossible to tickle yourself. Something about the way your nerves work prevents your body from sensing it as you would when someone else tickles you. It must be the same thing for this, because it feels a million times better with her doing the work than all the times I've done it myself put together.

I want to lie back and let it happen, to get lost in how she's making me feel, but I've heard that women complain a lot about guys being selfish. I reach over to her. It's at that moment I realize I have no idea what to do. I'd probably have more luck trying to read a Braille version of the Gutenberg Bible. They sure as hell don't teach the important stuff in sex-ed class.

"Here, like this," Jasmine says. She puts her hand over my fingers and moves them. When I start to get the hang of it, all the pressure I'm feeling disappears. I figure if I just do like she tells me, I can't go wrong, but it's not easy to concentrate when she's got me so distracted.

So I try to think about cards.

I imagine myself sitting at the final table of the World Series of Poker. All the Hold 'Em greats—Howard Lederer, Phil Ivey, Dan Negreanu, Annie Duke, Phil Hellmuth, Greg Raymer, and of course, Doyle Brunson—are there. I pick them off one by one until only the headphone-wearing Hellmuth is left. After a grueling battle, during which the lion's share of the chips shifts back and forth a bunch of times, I take Hellmuth down with my favorite hand, a suited jack-queen. My starting hand turns into two pairs on the flop and a full boat, jacks over queens, on the river. I slow-play the whole thing until Hellmuth goes all in on his triple queens. He storms off like he always does, mumbling under his breath, until it's just me with a gold bracelet, hundreds of flashbulbs, and a few million dollars.

I try to imagine what that moment would be like.

I try to put myself there . . .

And then I realize it's nothing compared with what I'm feeling right now at the edge of this pool. It's nothing compared with how connected I feel to this person.

Our lips and hands roam all over each other, and before long my brain feels like it's short-circuiting. I drop to my back. Jasmine collapses on the pool steps. Her cheeks are flushed. We're both exhausted—but in a really good way.

I try to lift my head.

It drops back to the tile.

Totally exhausted.

"Remember how I said you're cute?" Jasmine says.

"Uh-huh," is all I can manage.

"You're even cuter when my hand's in your soggy underwear."

She hops out of the pool and grabs a white towel from a rack designed to look like one of those Indian dream catchers. I watch her dry herself off.

She tosses me a towel.

"Thanks," I say.

After I dry off, Jasmine leads me to one of the recliners. She lays me down and stretches out alongside me. One of her legs overlaps mine, and she puts her head in the hollow part of my shoulder. I can feel the warmth of her body, and it calms me. Regardless of all the crap that's going to come down on me tomorrow, lying with her is enough.

We stay there for a while. I'm not sure how long, maybe a few minutes, but it's long enough for our hookup to settle into being the way it is. And I think we're both okay with it. It feels good.

"Let me ask you a question," I say.

Jasmine turns to me. Her mascara is so smudged she looks like she fell face-first into a bucket of shoe polish. I wipe her cheeks with the corner of my towel.

"You have really cool eyes," I say. "They're like green with brown streaks."

"That's not a question."

"Okay then, why do you hide your eyes with all that makeup?"

She sits up and unzips her duffel bag. She pulls out a large, leather-bound book and drops it on my lap. It lands so heavily I'm afraid it might cut off the circulation to my legs—or worse.

"What is this," I ask, "*War and Peace?*"

"It's my scrapbook. I said I'd let you look at it if you helped me with calculus."

"If it's private . . ."

She shrugs. "It's okay. Maybe it'll show you I'm not hiding anything."

Even with all the stuff that's happened between us today, it still feels way personal to look in Jasmine's scrapbook. It's a different kind of personal, the kind that sits someplace deep inside your chest and scrambles deeper at the first trace of light. I hesitate before opening the cover, but I do.

Each spread is more inspired than the last, as though she's been honing her scrapbooking skills page by page. It begins with Jasmine's childhood. Pictures of her as a bald baby, school photos with missing teeth (and one with big pink sunglasses), and pictures from various birthday parties and Christmases. Many of the photos are surrounded by captions like "Look at me!" and "If I knew then what I know now . . ." as well as intricately cut construction paper designs, stickers, and glitter.

I barely recognize Jasmine in some of the pictures—especially the ones before she started with all the eyeliner and hair dye. Her natural hair color is light brown. In some of the photos, the summer ones, she's closer to blond. Her hair went halfway down her back through seventh grade or so.

"Jasmine, this book is incredible."

Her back is to me, and her shoulders are all scrunched up.

"What's the matter?" I ask.

"It's weird when someone looks at it."

"I can put it down."

"No, it's okay," she says. "It's just weird."

I close the book. "What's weird about it?"

"I don't know," she says. "I feel like every page you turn is like peeling back another layer, until you're looking at the raw core."

I grab Jasmine's arm and pull her tight to me. The scrapbook is wedged between us like a brick. "But I like everything I see."

She smiles wide, one of those smiles where her cheeks pull so far away from the sides of her teeth they make a clicking sound. "You're just saying that because of the swimming lesson I just gave you."

I squeeze her tight. "That's only sixty percent of it."

"What's the other forty?"

"See? You *can* do math."

"Oh, shut up." Jasmine punches me playfully in the shoulder. She sits up and pulls her clothes next to her.

"Where're you going?"

She tugs off her underwear from beneath her towel and tucks it in her bag. She fishes her bra from the pool and wrings it out. Then she crosses the tile toward me and starts shimmying into her panty hose. "We'd better go find Scott."

GOLD RUSH
(a four and a nine)

I realize how big the hotel is when I get off on the sixth floor. Hallways stretch off in both directions and branch about a million different ways. I'm starting to be bothered by all of the Native American décor. I wonder if any real Native Americans have ever had a peach-and-seafoam-colored tepee like the one on the wall across from the elevator.

"We should split up," I tell Jasmine.

She nods and heads off in the direction of 651–699.

I take 601–650.

As I walk down the hall, I begin to whisper "Scott!" in one of those loud whispers that isn't really a whisper. I hear the *ding* of the elevator, and I spin around as the door slides open. Bourbon, the drunken guy from the poker room, staggers out and leans against the tepee painting. I'm one of those people who feel the need to straighten pictures when they're crooked, but the tepee is bolted to the wall.

"Hey, Chip," he mutters at me. His voice is so slurred I can barely make out the words. If I hadn't seen him down a bottle of Jack Daniel's with my own eyes, I'd think he was just acting drunk—and really exaggerating. "What're you doing on my floor?"

"Looking for a friend."

"Yeah, all these doors look the same." He pulls a key card from his pocket and holds it at arm's length. He peers at it like he's going to see something on it other than the casino logo. "What room am I in?" Bourbon jerks a thumb over his shoulder. It hovers in the air a second, then drops to his side. "I think it's this way."

"Here, let me help." I grab his card and start down the hallway, trying it in every door I come to. "Do you remember which side you're on?"

"Damned if I know." Bourbon trails after me, using the walls to hold himself upright. "Tina!" he shouts.

I tell him to be quiet and that I'll find the right room, figuring with a hundred rooms on the floor and around five seconds per door, it'll take me only eight or nine minutes to try them all. It's the least I can do after beating him out of a few hundred bucks tonight. I make my way from 601 through 615 and then start down the first branch, which leads to 616–630. Finally, on 629, I hear the familiar whir of a happy key card. The little green light flickers on, and I pop the door open a few inches.

Bourbon makes his way up behind me and lets the door-frame hold him up. "Thanks a million, Chip," he manages to say as his feet lead him into the room. "G'night."

I start back toward the main hallway to resume my search for Scott when I hear a crash and a clatter behind me.

"What the hell?" I hear Bourbon holler. The door flings open. The doorknob strikes the wall with a loud *thwong*, and Scott comes barreling out, wearing nothing but his boxers and one sock. His shoes are clutched under one arm.

"Bombs away!" he yells, and without a glance back he

pushes past me and piles into the stairwell. Scott hauls ass down the stairs faster than I could fully clothed.

Bourbon staggers out after him, bouncing off the wall across from his room. He lopes toward me and the door to the stairwell, but his anger is outweighed by his drunkenness. He catches a foot on the ice machine and takes a header into the maid's cart. "Get back here, you punk!" he yells from his knees, but Scott is long gone.

"The hell you looking at?" Bourbon says to me. "Get out of here." He staggers back toward the room.

"Tina!" he shouts. "Who the hell was that?"

"Serves you right, you jerk." A woman who I presume is Tina steps into the doorway wearing only a pair of black panties. She is pulling a white robe around her shoulders. "We came here for our anniversary, not so you could spend three days drunk in the casino. What happened to the sleigh ride you promised? The fancy dinners? The spa?"

"Goddammitall!" he screams even louder. He grabs a stack of bath towels from the maid's cart and hurls them at her, but they fall harmlessly short. Then Tina and Bourbon disappear into their room to continue the argument behind thin walls.

Jasmine comes up behind me. "What's going on?"

"Don't ask." I wave her toward the stairwell. "Scott's already downstairs. Just look for the panicky guy in the Sponge-Bob boxers."

Jasmine gives me a puzzled look and heads into the stairwell.

All of a sudden, Scott's clothes—actually, Mr. Amato's clothes—start flying out the doorway. The cobalt blue shirt and charcoal jacket smack against the opposite wall and drop to the ground. The khakis get hung up on the tip of a mounted mauve tomahawk.

Bourbon and Tina keep yelling. It will only be a matter of minutes before someone calls security. I grab Scott's threads and dart into the stairwell, leaving the shitstorm behind.

BEER HAND

(an unsuited two and seven)

As I catch up to them on the landing between the third and fourth floors, Jasmine is snapping photographs of Scott in his boxers. "This will make a great scrapbook page," she says between laughs.

"Hey, this isn't some kind of peep show!" Scott complains. He's doing his best to cover as much of himself as possible with his arms and one leg, but his efforts only make him look like a flamingo having a seizure. "Andrew, help!"

Even though I went down only two flights of stairs, I'm out of breath, probably because it's hard to breathe in the midst of all the laughter.

I toss Scott his clothes, and he leaps at them like a ravenous dog.

"So, what happened up there?" I ask.

"Isn't it obvious?"

"And here you are in all your splendor," Jasmine says, snapping another photo.

"Oh, shut up." Scott pulls up his pants and begins to work on his belt. "Anyhow, maybe I should be asking you guys the same question. Both of you have wet hair."

My eyes turn down, and my face feels like it's on fire.

Scott slaps me on the back with his free hand. "You dog!"

"You dog!" Jasmine mimics. "I know guys talk, but jeez, I'm standing right here."

"How'd you do in the poker room?" Scott asks me.

"Close to fifteen hundred."

"Damn, maybe you *could* make this a career move. I can be your manager."

"That's exactly what I don't need."

"Anyone see my other sock?" he asks.

Jasmine and I stare at him blankly.

"Oh, wait!" Scott fishes in his pocket and pulls out the pair of white athletic socks from his father's top drawer. "And you thought I was being stupid bringing these." He sits on the step and starts putting them on. "So, what do you want to do now?"

I think about the casino, the poker room. I think about Shushie's place. I think about sitting at one of those huge, green tables hour after hour. The rush I usually get playing poker is nothing compared with the rush I felt at the roof-top pool with Jasmine—or tearing down the stairs after Scott. For the first time in months, I feel alive. Going back down to sit with Harris, Polo, and Gold seems pointless—even stifling.

"You know what?" I say. "I think we should head back."

"Are you kidding me? With all that cash, we could have a blast. I want to learn how to play craps."

I count out five hundred dollars and tuck the bills into Scott's pocket.

"Hey, you only owe me two hundred."

"Call it even," I say. "It's the least I can do."

"Great. More to lose shooting dice!"

"And what happens when that drunk guy comes down and finds you?"

A smile creeps across Scott's face. "Good point. Let's head home."

The dark sky presses down on us, like the classroom ceiling when I went back to visit my kindergarten teacher a few years ago. Yoko hums along the highway in the melted ruts. Hardly a word passes between us, but no one suggests putting the music on. I don't know if it's because there's only so much Four Seasons you can take before your eardrums burst or because of something else. I suspect it's the *something else*.

The ride home always goes faster than the ride there, and I realize I don't want our trip to end. I consider suggesting we turn around and head west. I wonder how far we could get on fifteen hundred bucks. With gas prices where they are, not far in a 454.

Finally, Scott pokes his head between the front seats and breaks the silence. "Hey, Jasmine, let me ask you a question."

"Okay."

"What does being stoned feel like?"

"What?" The single word cuts through me like a chain saw through a stick of butter.

"You hang out with Jim, and he deals drugs. At least that's what I hear around school—"

"I don't do drugs. I've never done drugs."

Her answer surprises even me. I never saw Jasmine as a "druggie," but I figured she must have at least tried them a few times.

"Never?" Scott asks.

"I'm screwed up enough without that shit."

"But Jim—"

"Jim and I fight about it all the time. I hate hanging out with him when he's stoned. He's so different when he's straight—so . . ."

"So, what?" I say. It comes out a little too defensively, but she's talking about him like they're still dating.

Jasmine's fists clutch the steering wheel so tightly her knuckles poke up like there are marbles in her fingers. "Never mind."

"So what happens next?" Scott asks.

I shrug. "Nothing happens, I guess."

"What did you expect?" Jasmine says.

"I don't know," Scott says. "I expected *something* to change."

"Something did change," I say to him. "You sank to a new low on the sixth floor of the hotel."

Jasmine bursts out in laughter.

"That doesn't count."

"How about that you'll have to visit me in juvie for the next few years where I'll be hammering rocks and making macramé wall hangings?"

"You really think your dad called the police?" Jasmine asks me.

"Half the police force brings their uniforms to the cleaners. I'm sure he's called someone by now."

"I doubt it," Scott says.

"It'd be easier if he did. It would've been one thing if I ran away for the night, but I took Yoko. I stole from the cleaners and then I took Yoko."

"Actually, *I* took Yoko," Jasmine says. A clump of ice rattles around the wheel well like Yoko is voicing her own opinion. "You guys came along for the ride, which means you're only accessories."

"I'm taking the heat for this," I say to her. "We'll crash at Scott's. Tomorrow morning, I'll take you home and deal with my father alone."

"You couldn't drive this car to the end of my block without wrapping it around a tree," Jasmine says. "This rear-wheel drive is nuts in the snow."

"Watch me."

Neither of them protests again, and we spend the rest of the ride listening to the engine growl in harmony with the drone of the tires on the road.

"Oh shit," Scott says as Jasmine rolls up to his house.

"What?" I say.

"The driveway's shoveled."

"Good," Jasmine says. "It's easier for us to get in there."

"My dad must have shoveled before he went to Maggie's for the night. He's going to tear me a new one for not doing it."

"At least he's not here," I say. "I just hope he didn't look in the sock drawer."

"I don't care about that. I'll just tell him I borrowed his socks and the money dropped out when I was changing for gym class."

"Like he'll believe that," Jasmine says.

"Yeah, I know, but what's he going to say? We'll both know I'm lying, but there's nothing he can do to prove it. All the money's here."

Jasmine pulls into Scott's driveway, and the three of us go inside.

"Crash wherever you want," Scott says, heading toward his bedroom. "I'll catch you in the morning."

"It *is* the morning," I point out. "It's after three."

"Yeah, well, I have a history test to fail at nine, so I'll see you later."

Jasmine and I lay a fleece across the lumpy couch and gather a few pillows from the linen closet. I lie next to her, but I'm getting a weird vibe, like she's distant and mechanical—like her thoughts are somewhere else. She snuggles against me, but she says nothing. Her body is warm alongside mine, and her head is heavy on my chest. She sighs.

The television remote is wedged uncomfortably between us, but I leave it there. If I push her away, I'm afraid we'll never get this close again. I kiss her on the top of her head, like my mom still does when I'm sick, and within seconds I'm asleep.

BIG CHICK

(an ace and a queen)

My eyes open to a bright column of light that squeezes between the curtains. It reaches across the room and lands on a black duffel bag. All at once I remember where I am. Jasmine is pressed against me. Her head is still on my shoulder, and her rib cage gently rises and falls. I feel her light breath as it drifts across my cheek. My arm is numb, but I don't dare move it for fear of waking her. I don't want this to end.

Even from the other room, Scott's snoring practically rattles the windows. It's the same sound that used to keep me up when his parents were getting divorced. We would play Four Horsemen in his bedroom until dawn, then crash after a dozen sodas and a pound of frozen miniature Snickers bars. I would stare at the ceiling replaying the night's hands in my head—devising new strategies—but Scott would be asleep as soon as his head hit the pillow. Even with his parents hating each other in the next room, after a Four Horsemen marathon he could sleep better than a sloth on NyQuil.

I take a few seconds to drink it all in. I want to remember this moment—the first time I woke up with someone else next to me. I want to crystallize it in my brain so years from now I'll be able to recall every detail, down to the strands of Jasmine's black hair soaking in her own drool.

Jasmine sucks in a deep breath like something startled her. She lifts her head and wipes her face with her sleeve. She looks around, then up at me. "Hey," she says with a sleepy smile.

I try to pull her closer. I want to feel her arms around me again, but she pulls away. Fishhooks pierce sensitive and vital things inside my chest. She swings her feet to the floor and heads to the bathroom. Each step pulls the fishhooks a little more until all I can think of is trailing after her and asking what's wrong. But I don't; I let the fishhooks hurt.

The snoring stops and Scott walks into the living room. His hair on the left side of his head is sticking straight up, and his voice is so reedy with sleep that I barely recognize it. "What time is it?"

I glance at the clock through the archway in the kitchen. "Just before eight."

He peeks through the gap between the curtains, then claps them shut against the invading light. "I guess we can still make it to school."

"There's no way I'm going to school." I think about how my father freaked out yesterday when I told him I had taken the money from the register. I think about the stapler. My hand makes its way to my forehead. I can feel only traces of a bump and a small abrasion. I think about Yoko and how she's been sitting outside unprotected all night. "I have a lot to deal with today."

"I'll go with you."

"No way. I have to do this alone."

"I'm just as guilty as you."

"Shut up."

"This whole thing was my idea in the first place."

"What's the point?" I hear something in my voice that reminds me of Shushie telling me to stop playing poker. All I need is a newspaper to rattle and a Horny Bastard mug to complete the picture. "Put the money back in the sock drawer and walk away. You'll be Scott free."

We both smile at the lame joke, and Scott nods in acceptance.

"Dude," he whispers. His eyebrows waggle like two caterpillars under a magnifying glass. "What's going on with . . ." He flicks his head toward the bathroom door.

Jasmine's voice echoes from the bathroom. "I can hear you!"

Scott's eyes reach out to me imploringly.

I only shrug.

The toilet flushes, the water runs in the bathroom, and the door swings open. Jasmine is fully dressed, and her bag is loaded up. "Let's hit the road," she says. Her bag—scrapbook and everything—lands heavy on the couch, and it jostles me into action.

By the time we get outside, Scott's nosy neighbor, Mrs. Foster, is dragging her garbage cans to the side of her house. She's wearing a pink housecoat, black fur-topped snow boots, and a baby blue hat with a wooden fish dangling from the brim. Her eyes narrow in a scowl, and I think I can see a few new wrinkles spring up on her face.

Scott walks us to the car. "Well, dork, good luck with your father." He pokes my forehead with his finger. "And watch out for flying staple guns."

"Shut up."

"Catch you later, Jaz," Scott says.

"Later," she says back.

Scott bounds up the porch steps two at a time and flings open the front door. "Give me a jingle," he calls to me, making the universal sign for a telephone with his thumb and pinkie. "Let me know what happens."

"Is it morbid curiosity or do you really care?"

"What's the difference?"

I can't remember the last time I called Scott. For the last few months he's been doing all the work. I haven't been doing a damn thing. I promise myself to call.

Mrs. Foster abandons her garbage can in the middle of her driveway and shuffles to the curb. She inspects Yoko, Jasmine, and me like she's seen all three of us on *America's Most Wanted*. Hornets start buzzing in me. Were we on the local news last night? I can see the report: Local boy with stapler dent in his forehead has gone missing along with a Goth chick, a fantasy card game player, and a kick-ass muscle car.

The slush and salt on Yoko's sides make her seem gray. I wonder if car washes are open on Tuesday mornings in the middle of winter. Washing Yoko before we take her back might soften the blow for my father. I doubt it.

Mrs. Foster shakes her head, and her scowl gets even scowlier. I'm sure she's going to say something about the youth of today being shiftless and lazy. She's going to say how Jasmine and I should be in school. She's going to say how things were so different in "her day," when you could see three movies, twelve cartoons, and a newsreel for a nickel.

"What's the problem?" I snap at her.

Mrs. Foster peers at me over her glasses and then back down at Yoko. "You should not take such a magnificent car out in this weather." Her French accent is thick. She must be from Quebec. "The Chevrolet Chevelle SS four-fifty-four was one of the finest muscle cars ever made. This vehicle should be sheltered through winter. I have a few garages out back. Fifty dollars per month."

"No thanks. I'm taking her home now."

"Suit yourself," she says, adjusting the wooden fish on her hat so it hangs above her left eye. "But get that car inside soon."

"Yes, ma'am."

"What did she want?" Jasmine asks as we start the drive to her house.

"Someone to talk to."

Jasmine goes on to talk about her crazy neighbor across the street, her aunt's neighbor, and her neighbor when she was five years old. She's tossing around all this small talk because she doesn't know what to say. I know she has no idea what to say because I have no idea either. I count stop signs as we snake through the back streets to the other side of town. When the blocks get longer and the front yards get deeper, I know we're nearing Jasmine's house. One of us is going to have to say something.

Finally, I can't take it anymore. "So what happens now?"

Jasmine slows the car to a crawl. Then she stops in front of her house. "What do you think, Andrew?" She's got this annoyed edge in her voice, like I've just stepped on her cat for the fifth time.

"I don't know. I kind of figured—"

"You kind of figured what—that we'd start being boyfriend-girlfriend and start hanging out all the time with our hands in each other's back pockets and I'd start coming over for Sunday dinner?"

My face begins to burn, and I feel pressure behind my eyes. I look out the window and try to will the tears away, but they come anyway.

"I'm sorry, Andrew. I didn't mean that." Her voice softens, and her hand moves to mine. "I have a lot of things to sort out."

I wipe my tears with my free hand and notice a squirrel standing on the surface of the snow next to Jasmine's mailbox. He's nibbling on a stray acorn. Little bits of it fall to the ground.

"I have a lot of things to sort out," she says again.

"What, this Jim crap?" I take her hand and start massaging her fingers. "You can't help what happened."

Streaks of mascara trail down her face, branching and splitting like cracks in a shattered windshield. "But what I can help is bringing you into it." She pushes my hand away. "You're practically a genius, Andrew. Get out of this stupid town. Go to New York City or Boston or someplace else really cool. Take a few semesters abroad. Before long, you'll realize there's much better waiting for you. Someday you'll be thanking God you didn't get mixed up with me."

"Don't say that."

"It's true."

"So what are you going to do?" I say. "Are you going to run back to Jim? Are you going to jump from one asshole to another? Maybe you'll be one of those women who watches Oprah every day to feel better about your own shitty situation."

Her hands drop from the steering wheel. "I'm not going to be like that."

"Sure," I say. "I'll bet you call Jim as soon as you get inside."

She glares at me as if fire could blast out of her eyes. I want to wipe the black streaks from her cheeks, to take her round face in my hands and kiss every inch of it, but her expression makes Mrs. Foster's scowl look like a pussycat's. "And what makes you think you'd be any better for me?" she hisses. "You and Jim aren't so different. You're both equally fucked up. And given enough time, being with you would turn out the same as being with him. There'd be lies. There'd be resentment. The whole bucket of bullshit."

My throat tightens like a chunk of apple is wedged sideways in there. Finally I manage to get words out. "At least I'd never hit you."

"You know, that part doesn't even bother me anymore."

Jasmine is from a completely different world, one that I can't possibly understand. But I know I don't want to be without her. I need her.

"Jasmine—"

"No, Andrew. That's enough. I'm too tired. Drop her in gear and get Yoko home." She flings open the door, grabs her bag from the floor next to me, and runs up the driveway.

I want to chase after her, to make her understand how much I care for her—to make her really understand—but I'm frozen in the car as though my skin is sewn to the seat. Finally, I move over to the driver's seat and pull the door closed.

I turn on the stereo and turn it up all the way, but not even Frankie Valli's squeals can distract me from the pain. One more stop and then it's home to face my father.

F I D O
(a king and a nine)

The pool hall no longer looks like a fortress to me; it looks shabby. Melted snow runs down the roof into the clogged gutters. The overflow cascades onto a row of bushes barely clinging to life.

The defroster is going full blast, and the air it is kicking out smells like burnt hair. The windows are foggy and sweating. I make a few baby feet with my fist and think about Shaolin monks. They can get their heart rates down to thirty or forty beats per minute. Mine's going ten times that.

I wipe the tears from my face and get out of the car.

When I open the door to the pool hall, the heat blowers blast down on me. At the counter, Ruth puts down her egg sandwich and gives me a puzzled look as she chews. If poker has taught me one thing, it's to read faces. She knows that Shushie banned me.

"Hey," I say.

Ruth swallows her bite and lifts her cigarette from the ashtray. She takes a deep drag. "You know I can't let you downstairs, Andrew." As she speaks, the smoke hangs between her lips in a thick cloud.

"Tell him I just need a minute."

"Please, Andrew, don't make my job difficult."

"Come on. It's not like I'm an ax murderer or anything."

Her eyes move to the phone, then back to me. "I already know what he's going to say."

"Then let me sneak down. I'll tell him you were in the bathroom when I came in."

The shrill ringing of the phone interrupts her frown. Ruth lifts the receiver to her ear. "Uh-huh. Yeah. Okay." She hangs up and looks at me. "He says to let you on down."

"How did—"

She answers my question with an extended index finger. I follow where she's pointing and see a small black camera mounted in the corner. "Eye in the sky," she says.

"Has that always been there?"

Ruth shakes her head. "He had them installed yesterday."

"How come?"

"Shushie says you can never be too careful."

I head through the heavy steel door and down the stairs. The doorframe is chipped and scarred, and I wonder when the last time the place got a fresh coat of paint was. Probably never.

The smell of the poker room washes over me, and I take a deep breath. The place is empty with the exception of a small cluster of people at the corner table. Sam Barr, Mary Edwards, and a few guys I've never seen before. That corner table was always my favorite; it made me feel like a gangster.

My hand reflexively goes to my pocket. I feel for the thousand dollars I have left and step into Shushie's office.

"I only have a few minutes," he barks without looking up. His eyes are glued to the six brand-new monitors sitting on a metal stand next to his desk. "I've got to sit in on that game soon or Buzz and Louie are going to take off. The action is getting stale."

"Shushie, I—"

"And if this is about coming back, you can forget it—at least until you're eighteen."

"Would you let me get a word in for once?"

Shushie is not used to being snapped at, and he raises an eyebrow. The single motion of that eyebrow is enough to shut me up, and I slide into the seat across from him. This hulking man has acted like my mentor all these months, ever since I started playing here, but I wonder how well I really know him.

"Look, I just came by to ask you a question."

He considers me for a moment and nods.

"How did you beat me?"

He doesn't say anything, so I continue. "I got slaughtered these last few weeks, and it wasn't because of bad play. My game is better than ever. I replay hand after hand in my head, and nowhere did I screw up. You know me. I don't bluff and I don't tilt."

For the first time since I've walked in, Shushie's eyes leave the monitors. He looks squarely at me. It's a piercing stare, like he's trying to size me up, and it makes me squirm in my seat. He leans back in his chair, and it wails in protest. "I'm sure you've heard this saying about a thousand times—hell, I've said it to you before. I'll start you off." He sniffs hard and clears his throat like he's going to deliver the Gettysburg Address. "If you're sitting at the card table for a few minutes and you can't figure out who the sucker is . . ."

Shushie's right. I do know the saying, and I finish it for him, ". . . then it's you."

With a nod, he takes a bite of his doughnut. A glob of dark jelly plops to the desktop. I let his words sink in, hoping I might figure out what he's talking about. After a few moments, I still have no idea.

"Since you'll be out of my game for a few years," Shushie says with his mouth full, "I suppose it won't hurt to tell you."

My throat feels like it's closing up. "Tell me what?" I manage to say.

"You have a tell, Andrew."

"I have a tell?"

He nods. "Actually, you have a bunch of them."

I have no idea what to say. On the one hand, it explains how I blew through all my money so quickly. On the other, I feel completely betrayed by everyone I've been sitting at the tables with. I want to scream. I want to leap across the table and smack Shushie. And at the same time I want to crawl under a rock. They took advantage of me. They stole my money. They drove me to steal from my father's store.

"Who knows about this?" I ask.

"Just about everyone. You know how Matt can't keep his mouth shut. Once he caught on, he babbled about it all over the club. You know, 'Hey, did you see Andrew cross his arms after he didn't hit any of his outs on the river?' Shit like that."

"How long have you known?"

Shushie shrugs. "Since early on."

"You've been playing my tells, too?"

Shushie shrugs again; this time his shoulders practically

sandwich his ears. "What do you expect? It's part of the game."

My breathing goes short and choppy. I look down at my feet. My leg is pumping furiously just like Scott's does. I wonder if this is how he feels all the time. Even though the carpet is one of those tweedy numbers that's supposed to hide stains, I can see dark spots all around me.

I remind myself how I spent most of last night looking at Harris's cards. I found an edge, and I took it without the slightest remorse. And made money as a result. I know if I'd been in Shushie's position, I would have done the same thing. Poker is a game of angles, and he found an angle on me. Matt found it, too.

Shushie grabs a brown paper bag next to the phone and pulls out a foam cup. "You want a coffee? Sammy brought it for me earlier, but I want to learn how to use that damn coffeemaker."

I fold back the lid and take a sip. I've never tasted anything so bitter. I swallow it and take another. Straight coffee tastes nothing like the cappuccino drinks I'm used to.

"*Sonuvabitch!*" floats in from the poker room, and I know someone is having a run of bad cards. The hairs on my neck prickle up, and I want pull out my bankroll—to ask Shushie to play here just one more time. But the thought reminds me of a dog rolling on its back in submission. I wrap my hands around the coffee cup until it stings my palms. "What *are* my tells?" I ask. I'm talking to Shushie about myself like it's not me, like I'm some kind of case study—something to be learned from.

He shakes his head. "You name it. You cover your mouth when you bluff. You glance down at your stack when the card helps your hand. You never look at your cards when you're sitting on the nuts."

"I never look at my hand?" I say in disbelief.

"Not when you're sitting on the nuts. You move straight in, like nothing else in the world matters."

Shushie pops the rest of the doughnut into his mouth, and it disappears as fast as a fly falling victim to a frog's tongue. "Then there's how you handle your chips. When you're holding good cards, you stack your chips carefully, like you know you're going to be pulling them back in front of you. When you're holding garbage, you fire the chips out there and let them tumble all over the place. Andrew, let me tell you. You're a poker player's dream. It took those guys longer than I would have expected to figure you out."

"How come you didn't just come out of your cave and crush me?"

Shushie shrugs. "You can milk the cow and keep it around for a long time, or you can butcher it and eat really good for a few days. Me, I like milk." Shushie opens a drawer and removes a Lucite tray filled with chips. "Look, I gotta get out there. I have to do some whale hunting."

I take another sip of the coffee. My mother once told me it's an acquired taste, but I can't understand why anyone would put up with the flavor of coffee in the hope they might develop a liking for it down the road. I slide the cup away from me.

"Good luck, kiddo," Shushie says. The dental work along the sides of his molars glistens. "Keep in touch."

"Thanks, Shush."

He squeezes out from behind his desk and gets to his feet.

I stand, too, and make my way into the sea of tables with him. I know once I leave the poker room, it's likely I'll never see it again. I glance around and take it all in. The static on the muted television. The stained and faded felt. The low, oppressive ceiling. I don't want it to wither from my memory. I don't want my mind to smooth out all the rough details. I want to remember it just as it is.

Shushie is already sitting down at the table. "Let's get a game going here!" he says as he stacks his chips into neat piles. New money. New action. The energy whips up like a cyclone. I turn my back on them and head toward the door. No one in this room is going anywhere soon.

Q - T I P

(a queen and a ten)

My father's van isn't at the house. He must be at the dry cleaners. Of course he's at the dry cleaners. There's no one else there during the day other than the pressing guy, and Jules can barely speak English. Closing the store entirely would be suicide for the business. People need their clothes.

My death grip on the steering wheel slackens. This is going to be a lot easier without my father around.

I try to ease Yoko up the driveway as quietly as possible, but her monster engine betrays me like a tattletale sister. I shut off the car at the bottom of the driveway and get out. The front door of the house flies open, and my mother rushes out, wearing only sweats and slippers. Rooster trails right behind her.

"Andrew!" she calls. "Where in the hell have you been? I've called everyone." She sprints down the driveway, throws her arms around me, and hugs me tight. I shrink back, but she hangs on like if she lets go I might disappear again. "Where have you been?" She sobs it over and over.

I let myself sink into her arms. The longer she hugs me, the longer I don't have to say anything. Over her shoulder, I can see Rooster peering up at me. He has a look on his face that's part happy and part ready to cry. "Why are you going to make Mom pull out all her hair?" he asks.

My mother shushes him.

"I'm going to get her a wig for Christmas."

"Get in the house," my mother tells him. "You aren't wearing a jacket."

"Neither are you."

"Why don't we all go inside?" Mom says. As soon as Rooster heads back up the walk, my mother peels herself away from me and looks into my eyes. "What were you thinking?" she asks.

My gaze shifts to the ground, and she leads me to the house. Rooster heads for the family room, and my mother and I go to the kitchen. Mom fixes me a cup of hot chocolate without saying a word. Then she slides a small plate in front of me. I look down and see the cookie angel with the Red Hots halo and frosted wings she promised.

It's a boy angel. Mom loves to point out there are no female angels in the Bible.

"Dad told me what happened at the cleaners yesterday," she says. "I really let him have it." Her eyes move to my forehead, and she leans over and kisses the bump. "But stealing money and taking the car? It's not like you, Andrew."

"Mom, I don't want to talk about it."

"You have no choice."

I snap off the angel's halo and put it in my mouth. The Red Hots dance on my tongue and let me forget about the train wreck going on in my stomach for a few seconds.

"Look," she says. "Your father went too far and he knows

it, but when he comes home, we'll work through this—all three of us."

"You weren't so understanding when he hit you," I mumble, more to the cookie than to her.

My mother stifles a gasp, and it comes out sounding like she's choking on something. "You remember that?" she whispers.

"I remember staying at Grandma's for a few weeks. I remember you cursing under your breath that a man who hits his wife is a no-good coward."

"I didn't think you remembered." She smiles through foggy eyes. "Your father is not like he used to be. Things are different now."

"Yeah, now he hits his son."

"That's not fair."

"You're absolutely right, Mom," I snap at her. "He's a model freaking father."

"Dad works hard to provide for our family."

"How much does he get paid to coach girls' high school basketball?" I ask. "Nothing. But he's there every day while I'm at the stupid dry cleaners."

"Dad wants you to learn the business."

"Did you ever think that might not be what I want to do?"

She leans toward me, her face softening a little. "Why did you take the money, Andrew? It's not because you don't want to work at the cleaners."

The moment is here. I can't avoid it any longer. I know this will be so much easier without my father around to yell and scream and throw staplers, but how do I start? What do I say? How much do I tell her?

Mom, I've been playing some cards here and there.

Mom, everything is okay now that I know what my tells are.

Mom, I stole money from the dry cleaners and tried to unload a bagful of crack to a junkie to make back some lost ground and then I stole a car so I could play poker at an Indian casino.

I think about the players at the club and how they've been feeding on my bankroll like a group of ravenous sharks, nipping and snapping and whittling away at me, never once thinking about how it might hurt me. Then my shoulders sag. They didn't take my money. I lost it. And I showed them how. I practically led them by the hand to my piggy bank and gave them sledgehammers and burlap sacks.

I burned through all my savings playing poker.

I tried to sell crack to get more money to play.

I tried to steal from my best friend.

I did steal from my own family.

Jasmine was right. I am no better than Jim.

I'm worse.

A chill works its way up my spine. My mother's hand comes alive, like she knows how I'm feeling and can massage it out of me. I look down at the angel and break off a wing.

My silence seems to make my mother even more nervous. Her hand leaves my shoulders, and she crosses her arms. "Andrew, you've got to tell me."

I fight back my tears. "I've been spending time at Shushie Spiegel's place," I finally say.

I don't expect her to understand, but just saying it takes ten thousand pounds off me. I exhale deeper than I have for months. All the stale air rushes out, and I fill my lungs with kitchen air, the smell of brown sugar and pancakes, of tacos and banana bread.

"Shushie Spiegel's place?" she whispers, as though saying it too loud will awaken some ancient curse. Her hand drops to the counter.

"I've been playing cards—poker actually—down in the basement." I break the other wing off the cookie. Without his halo or wings, the cookie just looks like a regular gingerbread man.

"And you took the money from the register to play?"

I nod. A single tear escapes and blazes a trail down my face. I drag my cheek across my shoulder.

My mother moves across the counter from me and lowers her head so she's directly in my line of sight. "Look in my eyes and tell me you haven't been doing drugs. I've heard things about that Shushie Spiegel."

I look in her eyes and say it: "I haven't been doing drugs, not even once."

"Swear to me."

"I swear."

It's strange my mother is so concerned about me doing drugs. I can't imagine anything having as strong a pull on me as playing cards. Standing in the poker club for that last time felt like I was hammering nails into my own coffin. I can't imagine my life without it.

Mom looks down at the counter and traces the edge of the Formica with her fingers. We both let time pass. Then her head perks up, like when a cat hears the can opener. Her attention swings to the doorway. "Rooster, get back in the family room."

"What're you guys talking about?"

"Nothing," she says. "I'll be right in with some juice. There's a new *Jimmy Neutron* on the TiVo."

"You guys never let me hear the good stuff."

"It's boring stuff," she says.

"Is Andrew in big fat trouble?"

"Just go on, Roo. I'll be right there." Rooster disappears through the swinging doors, and I hear the familiar chirp of the TiVo as he scrolls through the menus.

"Andrew, you have to promise me you'll stay away from Shushie Spiegel."

"I promise." I push the uneaten part of the cookie away from me.

"Go on upstairs and wash up," Mom says. She squeezes my shoulder, and it feels really good. "I'll call Dad."

Going to my room feels like a death sentence. Even the air weighs heavily in my chest. I feel for the thousand dollars in my pocket. Ten bills. I never thought something so light could feel so heavy, like the small pieces of green paper could drag me to the depths of the ocean. I hope the money will help put me back in my father's good graces; it'll more than cover what I took. Even a death row inmate has a chance for a reprieve. I place the bills on my desk next to the broken nutcracker soldier and change into jeans and a T-shirt.

Waiting for my father reminds me of waiting for the nurse to come in with my booster shots. My breathing is short, my shoulders are all hunched up, and I have no idea what to do. I pace back and forth, then sit at my desk and turn the nutcracker over in my hands a few times. His jaw is split down the middle, and his arm is cracked at the shoulder joint. It was less than a week ago that I broke him with Rooster's Slinky. It feels so much longer. I grab the wood glue from my drawer and get to work. After I mend the jaw and reattach the arm, I wrap him in rubber bands and stand him up on my tall dresser. He looks fine, but his mouth will never open again, and his left arm will be stuck at his side forever.

My grandfather gave me the nutcracker the winter before he died. I remember he warned me never to crack an actual nut with it because the jaw was too delicate. I always wondered what good a nutcracker is if it can't do its job. Only now do I realize the nutcracker has a more important duty. He's a soldier. He stands guard.

I admire the soldier for a moment. Then my eyes shift to my computer monitor. I jiggle my mouse to kill the screen saver. I move all of the poker-related icons and links into the Recycle Bin and uninstall the online poker game I've been playing. My pointer hovers over the Delete button. Finally, I click.

The thousand dollars stares at me from my blotter, and I realize the money won't make things better with my father at all. This has nothing to do with money. It has to do with trust. It has to do with responsibility and accountability. It has to do with family.

I grab the money and go down the hall to Rooster's room. His walls are covered from floor to ceiling with superhero posters. Taped over a scene of Spider-Man creeping up a brick wall is a single photograph. The photo is one I know well. It was the first time I let Rooster take a picture. Two summers ago he had been begging incessantly to use my camera. I asked him what he wanted to take a picture of, and he said, "I don't know, something I want to remember." When I put the camera in his hands and showed him which button to push, he told me where to stand. Before I got there, Rooster snapped the photograph. The result was a picture of me in a twisted position somewhere between walking to the side of the house and lurching back to tell him not to press the button until I was ready. My mouth is half open and my eyes are rolled up into my skull. Rooster handed me back the camera and ran off laughing. I gave him the print and never gave it much thought until now. Now I realize it's a very important photo—Rooster put me *on top of* Spider-Man.

I fold the bills twice and slide them into Rooster's piggy bank. Years from now, when he cracks the bank open, all of this will be ancient history. I'll pay my father back some other way.

S A I L B O A T S

(two fours)

think I hear my father's van pulling in. I leap to the window and
look outside. False alarm. It's only the UPS truck. Yoko is
still sitting at the bottom of the driveway. Salt and dirt cake
her sides so badly that she looks like an old beater—something ready for the car crusher. My father's going to freak out
when he gets home. And no matter how angry and upset I am
about what he did to me, I can't help but feel guilty. My father
pours himself into that car—Rooster does, too—and I took
Yoko out like I was borrowing an old bike.

I feel the urge to run out there and pull Yoko into the
garage—to polish her until she shines, but I know it's too late.
My father will be home any minute.

I collapse into my chair and look around for something to
do. I tuck the wood glue back into the top desk drawer and
arrange my pens and pencils so that all the pens are in one
mug and all the pencils are in the other.

Then I hear the van. And this time it's no false alarm. I
recognize the rattling sound it's made for years and that
squeak of the brakes that happens when it's cold out. I peer
between the slats of the blind. Seeing our Big Red Gro-
cery Getter pull up feels like a kick in the face with a soccer
cleat.

My father leaves the van in front of the house with the hazard lights blinking. He walks with an urgency that's somewhere between a trot and a run. I don't think I've ever seen him move so fast, and it makes me shrink back into my room as though he could reach right up and slap me from the curb. He squeezes between Yoko and the snowbank and darts up the front walk. White puffs leave his mouth, visible in the air like dragon's breath. I want to hide in the closet, maybe under the bed. I wonder if there's enough snow to break my fall if I have to jump.

Then it occurs to me. He didn't look at Yoko. He didn't even cast a single glance at her. My father ran right past his perfect, pristine car that now looks as though it's been left for years in a salt mine. My poker tell comes to mind—the one Shushie told me about. He said I never look at my cards when I'm sitting on the nuts. He said I move straight in, like nothing else in the world matters.

I sit down on the edge of my bed. The rubber-band-bound nutcracker soldier stares at me, that toothy, unmoving grin painted across his face.

The front door slams, and I hear the muffled sounds of my parents talking downstairs. I catch a glimpse of myself in the mirror over my dresser. With my messy hair and a few days' worth of high schooler stubble, I barely recognize myself. I sit up straight and gaze into my own eyes, hoping to prepare myself for whatever comes through the door.

Heavy footsteps take the stairs two at a time, then make their way down the hall. After two cursory knocks, the door pops open, and my gaze swings from the mirror to my father. It startles me how much I'm getting to look like him. Then I see the worry in his face—the deep lines like chasms, his eyes turning down at the sides. I've never seen him look like that, so grave, so weighed down. He's looking at me like nothing else in the world matters.

He charges at me and throws his arms around my shoulders. My mother comes in behind him and leans on the doorframe. Tears fill her eyes like she's reading one of the Hallmark cards from that drawer I'm not supposed to go in. Rooster squeezes his head between my mother and the door, and looks at me like he expects to see a train wreck. When he realizes it's just a hug, he pulls his head from the room and heads back downstairs.

I let my father hug me as long as he likes. Finally, my hands make their way around him. I feel his body shake, almost quiver, and the weight of him presses down on me, as if, if I let go, he'd collapse to the floor like a pile of rags. I let him lean on me, and I squeeze him tighter. My eyes meet my mother's. Her lips press together so hard they turn white, and she raises a hand until her fingers cover her mouth.

My hug seems to breathe new life into my father. His shoulders broaden and he sucks in a deep breath of air. And all at once I realize that everything is going to be fine between Dad and me.

OVER AND OUT
(a ten and a four)

How much did we make tonight?" I ask Scott as I organize the blue and white chips in the case. It's been three months since our trip to Crystal Waters, and that night gave us a lot of ideas. It was four hundred dollars to get the chips made, but it's the only way to make sure people don't bring their own into our game. I smile at the emblem we designed: a 1970 Chevelle with the name "Yoko" printed underneath.

"Now you screwed up my count," Scott says, dropping a handful of cash on the table in frustration. "Don't distract me."

Like I promised my folks, I haven't played a hand since we left Crystal Waters. I've dealt a whole lot, though. With Scott's house empty every weekend, it was the perfect place to start a poker club of our own. We run a $3–$6 game for high school students only. Between my knowledge of the game and Scott's entrepreneurial spirit, we're doing great.

"Six hundred and forty buckeroos," Scott says. "That's three twenty each."

I stuff the cash into my pocket and snap the lid of the chip case closed. After my father told me how he almost lost the business betting on football when I was a kid, I've been extra careful to stay out of the action. Running the club is easier money anyway. We charge a six-dollar sitting fee, and everyone has to kick in a big blind at the top of each hour. That's around fifty dollars per hour with a full table—and filling a table hasn't been a problem. Scott and I have actually been talking about starting up a second one once he learns to deal. The interest is certainly there.

Scott turns off his iPod, killing the casino mix we made, and turns on some hip-hop video channel on cable. I still can't get into hip-hop.

Even though I'm pulling in a ton of money, I'm still working at the cleaners to pay my father back. I don't think he'd smile on me slinging cards—even if I'm not playing. Between what I pinched from the register and what it cost to get the dings out of Yoko, it'll take me another two months, but after that he's agreed to let me quit.

My mom is happy because I'm so into Sudoku now. After I tore through every Sudoku book and mastered anything I could find online, she found a local club that does them along with other logic puzzles. Dorky, yes, but it keeps her happy. My first tournament, sponsored by the *Post*, is next weekend.

As for the money I'm making running the club with Scott, I'm socking it away for college. And maybe to buy a muscle car of my own down the road. Yoko really is a sweet ride.

Scott leaps to his feet and starts shaking his backside like he's grabbed an electric fence. "How the hell do those girls do it?" he asks.

"What girls?"

He points to the television. "You know, girls in rap videos who rattle their asses like jackhammers."

"I'm sure I have no idea."

"Can Jasmine do it?"

"Shut up."

"No, seriously. Maybe it's a genetic thing. Maybe it's linked to that second X chromosome."

"Why don't you ask her yourself?"

"You going to make a move soon or what?" he asks. "You guys already hooked up at the casino, and that was a long time ago."

My face gets hot. "She told me to back off."

"Dude, if you backed off any further, you'd be past Pluto."

"Pluto's not a planet anymore."

"Who cares?" Scott says. "It's still freaking far."

I don't expect Scott to understand, and I'm not going to waste time trying to explain. After our blowout in the car, I thought Jasmine and I were finished before we ever started. I'm just pumped that she called a few days later. She told me she didn't know what she wanted, that she was really confused, but she's managed to stay away from Jim and hasn't been dating anyone else. I don't want to screw anything up.

A knock sounds at the door. Scott and I both freeze. The porch light is off, and all of our regulars know what that means—either we're closed for the night or there's no room at the table.

"Shoot," Scott says, hitting Mute on the remote. "Probably Mrs. Foster from next door again."

I open the door. It's Jasmine. She's silhouetted by the streetlight behind her. She moves forward without a word and throws her arms around me. Her fruity smell intoxicates me, and her mouth finds mine like my teeth are magnets pulling at her tongue barbell. I stumble back a few steps, but she holds on.

"Jeez," Scott says. "How do I get a house call like that?"

"I think your right hand's waiting for you in your room," Jasmine says.

"I'm a lefty," Scott says. "Are we all still on for breakfast at eleven?"

"Better make it noon," Jasmine says. "You'll still make it to your Four Horsies tournament. I promise."

After Scott disappears into his room, Jasmine grabs the fleece blanket from the back of the couch and pulls me next to her. She turns her head to mine. She looks hungry.

No, starved.

"What's going on?" I ask her.

"I figured you would've made a move by now," she says. "Hell, we already hooked up at the casino."

I hear an "I told you so!" from behind Scott's closed bed-room door.

I grab the cable remote and turn the sound back on to drown out any more noise we might make. Jasmine leans in and kisses me. I think back to my Guy Meets Girl Algorithm. Somehow, whatever logic I employed at the time to create it seems flawed—seems completely ridiculous.

We both lie back on the couch. I suppose I could grow to like hip-hop after all.